WORKING FOR THE CEO

CEO SERIES BOOK 2

EMILY HAYES

1

Alice carefully inserted the key into the lock of her front door and slowly turned it, trying her best not to make a sound. Just as she closed the door behind her, she could hear her landlord rushing up the stairs. She held her breath as he knocked on her door.

"I know you're in there!" the landlord yelled through the door.

Alice looked down at the tub of Ben & Jerry's that was starting to melt in her hand but didn't dare move.

"If I don't get your rent by Friday, you will be evicted." And with that, the landlord stomped down the stairs again.

Grabbing a spoon from the kitchen drawer, Alice sat down on the kitchen floor. She knew that the somewhat melted Cherry Garcia was not the solution to her problems, but she needed the comfort and knew it was a better option than opening a bottle of wine at 10am to drown her sorrows.

Alice looked at the party invitation on her fridge. It was her best friend's birthday this weekend. Initially, she was looking forward to going out with her friends, but right now all she wanted to do was stay in bed and avoid the world.

This morning Alice had been fired from her latest, shitty job as a barista. The tiny wage she was paid was not enough to keep her from mouthing off to the narcissistic customer unhappy with her coffee being too hot.

The last thing Alice needed was to be fired. She was planning on using this week's wage and tips to pay her landlord as her rent was already way overdue. She couldn't really afford to spend any money on junk food like the Ben & Jerry's, but for now, she ignored the empty cupboards staring back at her.

Alice took another spoonful of ice cream when her phone vibrated in her pocket. It was Max, her best friend. "Hi Max," she answered with a mouthful of ice cream.

"What's wrong?" Max immediately picked up on her tone. Sometimes Alice thought that Max knew her better than she knew herself. They have been friends for almost ten years and not a single day went by without the two of them talking.

Alice let out a big sigh and said, "Guess who just joined the unemployed today?"

"What did you do this time, Alice?" Max asked already knowing that she was the cause of her own dismissal.

"I didn't do anything. It's not my fault some entitled uppity snob didn't have any common sense to realize that coffee is hot and can burn your mouth." Alice realized that she probably shouldn't have mouthed off to the customer but for as long as she could remember, she had no filter. Growing up, her parents and teachers had their hands full, but Alice never quite knew when to hold her tongue.

"Are you okay, hun?" Max asked, concerned.

"Guess I have to be. I'll wallow in my misery for a day and then start looking for something else tomorrow," Alice replied on the verge of tears.

"I'm coming over. Make sure to save me some ice cream," Max said knowing that Alice would be trying to find comfort in Cherry Garcia. Max disconnected the call before Alice could argue.

Alice looked down at the nearly empty ice cream tub in her hand. "Too late for that, Maxie," she said to herself.

She got up from the floor and decided to change into something more comfortable. Alice got dressed in an oversized hoodie that her latest ex-girlfriend left behind. At least something good came from their terrible relationship. It was a small blessing as she didn't have any money to spend on new clothes right now and her wardrobe was almost non-existent.

Her small studio apartment was messy, but she didn't have the energy to deal with that right now. Since she didn't have a job to go to anymore, she would have more than enough time to clean up her apartment.

Just as she was about to make herself comfortable on her futon, her front door opened and Max walked in without knocking. He was carrying two decadent frappes with whipped cream and drizzled caramel.

"You know you really should keep your front door locked," Max said as he plopped down next to Alice, handing her one of the drinks.

Rolling her eyes, Alice replied, "But then how would you get in?"

"I do know how to knock," Max said in his usual dramatic way. "Come here." He pulled Alice close. "You'll be okay, love."

Alice couldn't hold back her tears any longer. "I don't know what to do, Max. I'm 29 and still haven't found someone to settle down with, I have no job, and I'm being evicted on Friday. This is not how I imagined my life to be."

"It will all be okay, I promise," Max said as he tried to comfort Alice. "You are a fighter. A warrior. I know you will get through this. I might not be able to help with your financial issues, but I can help you find someone. Maybe you just need to get laid. Did you consider that?"

"I'm not in the mood to go out, Max," Alice quickly said as she wiped her eyes with her sleeve.

"We don't have to go out, silly. Look, here's a new dating app I found. You always cheer up when you get laid." Max showed Alice the latest dating app on his phone.

Alice rolled her eyes. "You know I tried those before, Max, and nothing good has ever come from it. It's all just a bunch of liars, catfish and freaks. Name one woman that I met on a dating app that was not one of those?"

Max grabbed Alice's phone from the table. "That's in the past, and this is a brand new app and you haven't tried this one yet. Let me help you set up your profile. Why don't you go get us some of that ice cream while I begin?"

"Yeah...about that..." Alice said with an innocent smile.

Max rolled his eyes. "It's fine, I should have known better than to expect you not to finish the tub in the state you are in. Let's get started and find you a playmate."

Although Alice appreciated Max trying to distract her form her current situation, she honestly didn't feel like scrolling through profiles just to start another cycle of hurtful breakups. Alice was terrible at relationships, that was a fact.

"You know you don't have to get involved with anyone you meet online, right? It can just be a quick fuck and left at that. You lesbians do like to overcomplicate things." Max said as he added photos to her new profile.

"You mean I should be more like you?" Alice giggled.

"I'm offended," Max said overdramatically. "Trust me, hun, you can have fun without emotional attachments. Why do you think my heart is still intact?"

"Because you don't have one?" Alice teased.

"Shut up," Max said as he handed Alice her phone back.

Alice was still unsure if this was a good idea, but Max was staring at her, eager for her to start swiping.

"Thanks, Max, maybe I'll go through it later. For now, why don't we watch a movie and just relax?" Alice said.

"Sure, sis, it's your choice today." Max kicked off his shoes and made himself comfortable.

Max was the best friend Alice ever had. She was grateful for his friendship and couldn't imagine her life without him.

As the opening scene of the movie started, Alice stared at her phone lying on the futon next to her. Maybe Max was right, maybe a no-strings-attached scenario was just what she needed to keep her distracted from her disastrous life. To be honest, any distraction would be good. She made up her mind that as soon as Max left, she would check her phone and see where this new app might lead.

2

Joanne Morgan was looking at the city skyline from her corner office as the head of HR was blabbing on behind her. It was a crisp fall day and Joanne was overwhelmed with deadlines she had to meet before Thanksgiving Weekend. She planned to take her private jet to visit friends in Martha's Vineyard. Of course, she could drive but that would just mean she would have even less time for work.

"Joanne, this is the third personal assistant that walked out in two weeks. You have to admit that having such a high staff turnover reflects badly on the company, especially when it involves someone in your position," the HR manager said.

"It's not my fault that you appoint spineless slackers, Kevin. All I know is that I need a new PA as soon as possible and you better find me someone who doesn't need to be spoon fed or who needs to be treated with kid gloves," Joanne said as her Manolo Blahnik stilettoes carried her to a seat at her desk.

"We have been through all the recruitment agencies

and they are hesitant to send us any recommendations because of your track record. It's going to talk a lot of smooth talking for them to send more recruits," Kevin said.

"In case you have forgotten, I am the CEO of this company. I can't babysit someone when I need them to be my right hand. If you don't mind, I have to prepare for my board meeting this afternoon since I have no one capable to assist me. Find me a new PA by the end of the day, Kevin. You're excused," Joanne said, shooing the HR manager away with her perfectly manicured hand.

Without a word, the HR manager got up and closed the door behind him. Joanne let out an exasperated sigh. She had no time for incompetence. She worked hard in her position as CEO, especially in a corporate environment that still favored men in executive positions. She knew that her misogynistic colleagues would use the tiniest mistake to turn against her.

As a successful businesswoman, she had to work twice as hard for the same recognition as her male counterparts. Her ex-wife could never understand that. A few years ago, Joanne's now-ex gave her an ultimatum. Either she cuts down on her working hours or she agrees to a divorce. It was an easy decision for Joanne. She already devoted so much of her life to her career that she could not give up her position as CEO. Honestly, alimony was a small price to pay for a successful career.

Joanne felt tense. She wasn't the type of woman to unwind by engaging in hobbies or sport. That would require commitment—which was something she didn't have time for. Usually Joanne would unwind by hooking up with a younger woman she would find on a dating up. It was much easier than having to go out and mingle, or god forbid, having to go on dragged-out dates only to go home alone.

She tapped on the dating app icon on her phone to search for someone who could help her unwind for the night. She never had any problems finding a partner. Joanne was not your average fifty-year-old woman. She oozed sex appeal and she knew it.

Joanne preferred spending time with younger women. They had less baggage, and with her looks and impressive lifestyle, it was easy to get them into her bed. Sure, she had a few clingy ones who couldn't accept the no-strings-attached agreement, but Joanne never had any problems brutally turning them away.

She started scrolling through the updated profiles, ignoring her inbox for now. She was the one that would initiate contact. If all else failed, she might go back and see if any of the messages she received was worth replying to, but she preferred getting a woman she wanted rather than settling.

As she scrolled through the possible one-night stands, a cute redhead caught her eye. Hopefully this one wasn't looking for her happily ever after. She opened the profile and was happy to see that there was no obvious red flags in the about me section.

Joanne was immediately attracted to the redhead's beautiful body. She was small and petite and her cute pixie cut highlighted her gorgeous green eyes and high cheek bones. In one of the pictures, the redhead was kite surfing in a barely-there bikini that left very little to the imagination. Joanne knew she found the right girl to spend the night with and decided to message her.

I like what I see in your pictures and I would like it if you could join me for a mind-blowing evening with no strings attached. There is a stunning view from my penthouse and I'll have the hot tub ready for us to relax in.

Joanne preferred getting straight to the point. Every woman she contacted knew exactly where they stood from the beginning. No one could blame her for leading them on. Either they wanted to join her or they didn't, she would not grovel or work to get someone into her bed.

More often than not, mentioning her luxurious lifestyle helped seal the deal, especially with much younger women. She didn't care that these women were impressed with her wealth as they wouldn't be around long enough to take advantage of it anyways.

She looked at the redhead's profile picture one last time before she placed her phone back on her desk and pulled up the reports she needed for her meeting on her big screen. She'd check back on the app once she was done with the meeting, but for now she needed to focus and get her meeting prep done.

An unexpected knock at her door startled her. "Yes," Joanne answered.

A mousy intern poked his head around the half opened door. "Excuse me, Miss Morgan, I have a message from Mr. Peterson."

"Go on," Joanne said, irritated with the skittish intern wasting her time.

The intern took a deep breath. "He said that one of the investors can't attend today's meeting due to his son's Junior League baseball game and that he will let you know which date they are rescheduling to."

"Seriously? They cancelled the board meeting for some kid's baseball game? Do they know how much time they had me waste and how many other appointments I had to postpone for today?" Joanne said as she stared at the intern with laser eyes.

"I, um, I'm sorry, Miss Morgan. I will let you know as soon as I can when the meeting will take place," the intern stammered.

"Fine," Joanne said, and with that she turned her chair around, letting the intern know that she was done with the conversation.

The intern closed the door behind him and Joanne got up to pace around. She was even more wound up than before. She couldn't believe that the board agreed to postpone their meeting. Surely the world didn't stop every time there was some kid's sporting event?

Right at that moment, she heard a notification from her phone. Hopefully it was the redhead replying to her message. If not, Joanne would find a distraction elsewhere. All she knew was that she had a lot of frustration ready to unleash on whoever would be joining her tonight.

3

Halfway through the movie, Max had to leave. He had snuck away from work to check up on Alice and had to get back before his boss returned from his weekly marriage counseling session. Max was certain that these sessions did more harm than good as his boss always returned to work in an even worse mood.

Not in the mood to watch the movie alone, Alice closed her laptop and picked up her phone. She noticed a notification from the new dating app that Max installed. She opened the app to read the message.

I like what I see in your pictures and I would like it if you could join me for a mind-blowing evening with no strings attached. There is a stunning view from my penthouse and I'll have the hot tub ready for us to relax in.

Alice was shocked by how forward and direct the message was. She wasn't use to someone saying they are looking for fun and nothing more. Usually the women she corresponded with online were all charming and flirty.

She opened the writer's profile and was surprised by

the beautiful, tall woman staring back at her. Alice wasn't sure what she was expecting, but it wasn't the type of woman she was looking at. This woman looked like an ice queen with white blonde, slicked back hair. Her blue eyes were piercing and looking at the ice queen, Alice knew that this was the type of woman who didn't take shit from anyone.

The ice queen was a bit older than the women Alice would usually go for. She wasn't sure if it would be a good idea, but Max's voice telling her to take a chance and have some fun was overpowering her own inner voice trying to convince her otherwise.

Alice swiped through the ice queen's photos. It was clear that this woman lived a life of luxury with her perfectly manicured hands and perfect long blonde hair. One thing Alice couldn't deny was how incredibly sexy this woman was.

For a moment, Alice thought that maybe it would be best to ignore the message and just get into bed, but then she realized she literally had nothing to lose. Joining a wealthy, sexy, older woman in her penthouse for a fun evening was definitely better than sitting around here sulking for the rest of the day.

She opened the message again and replied, *A hot tub with a view sounds like a great evening. I'd like to join you tonight.*

Even though Alice was still bummed, she was feeling a little excited for tonight. She immediately received a reply. *Good. I'll send you the location. Be sure to wear your shortest, tightest skirt with your highest heels. See you at 8pm.*

Alice looked down at her phone screen in confusion. It was the first time anyone had ever asked her to wear something specific to a date. She strangely liked how it felt. This woman was so bossy! She immediately flung open her closet to find something suitable.

She couldn't remember the last time she dressed up this provocatively but found a skirt in the back of her closet that she hadn't worn in years. Alice prayed it would still fit. She grabbed everything she needed and laid it out on the futon. Since she didn't have a lot of other short skirt/high heels options in her wardrobe, it would have to do.

With so much time to kill, Alice drew herself a hot bubble bath to relax in with a full face mask. She also had to fix her chipped nail polish and was glad that she would have time to spare.

She had to tell Max about her date. She called him on speakerphone as she lay back in the bubbles.

"Hey you," Max answered. "Feeling better?"

"Yeah, I suppose you could say that. I just thought I'd call to tell you I have a date tonight." Alice said as she looked down at her feet sticking out at the edge of her small tub.

"Really? When did this happen?" Max was clearly surprised at the news.

"I received a message on the app you installed this morning- a one night thing- no strings. *And,* she has a hot tub in her penthouse apartment!" Alice said.

"That must be a new record offer. The lesbians round here are improving! I'll drop by after work to help you with your outfit," Max excitedly said.

Alice knew how much Max enjoyed dressing her up. She was like his personal living Barbie doll, but she didn't mind. Her sense of style wasn't necessarily the best.

Quickly Alice replied, "No need. She told me what she

wants me to wear. I have it covered; I just hope I still fit into these clothes."

"She did *what*?!" Max was being super loud.

"She told me what she would like me to wear tonight. Why are you freaking out over it?"

Max seemed momentarily lost for words but then he asked, "Alice, hun, you don't think that's weird?"

Glaring at her phone Alice replied, "You were the one that said I should throw caution to the wind, Max. That's what I'm doing."

"I know, it's just a little *well, kinky,* that's all. Where are you going for your date?" Max quickly asked.

"She invited me to her place and—"

"She sounds like some bossy bitch right there, be careful, ok?" Max cut her off.

"It will be fine, Max. I'll send you the location and I'll be sure to check in with you, okay?" Alice said, rolling her eyes.

"You better. I'll be waiting for the location. I better go now; the boss is in another terrible mood. Remind me never to get married, okay?" Max said.

"I will. Bye, Maxie, Love ya." Alice didn't want anything to ruin her excitement. She laid back and stared at the bathroom ceiling, ignoring the peeling paint in the corner.

Tonight, she would let go; she would wear what she was told, she would have amazing sex with the Ice Queen, she would be free of all responsibilities and worries. Tomorrow she would start searching for a new job and return to her mundane, adult existence.

∽

JOANNE WAS WALKING along the deck of her penthouse apartment to ensure everything was ready for the night. As usual, her housekeeper didn't disappoint her. The fireplace was already lit and the hot tub was set to the perfect temperature.

Throughout the afternoon, she imagined all the things she wanted to do to the little redhead coming over. She just hoped that it wouldn't take hours of small talk to get her naked and into her bed.

Joanne was dressed in a sexy, black, low-cut catsuit. She knew that the design flattered her in all the right places and was proud of how it accentuated her voluptuous ass.

"Excuse me, Miss Morgan, your guest has arrived. She is waiting in the foyer," her housekeeper announced.

"Thank you, I'll be right there." Walking towards her apartment entrance, she gave herself one last look over in the mirror, ensuring her perfect makeup and cherry red lips didn't need any touch ups.

She was pleasantly surprised by the redhead standing in her apartment. She was dressed as instructed and it looked like her skirt was one size too small, but that only turned Joanne on even more.

"Good evening, I'm Joanne," she said, looking the redhead straight in the eye.

"Hi Joanne, I'm Alice," the redhead said with a seductive smile.

"Shall we go sit outside?" Joanne invited her to the deck.

Just as they reached the deck, Alice said, "If you don't mind, I need to check in with a friend first. I don't want to be disturbed during our evening."

Joanne started laughing. "That's cute, you still need a

babysitter."

The redhead gave her an angry glare. "I might look young, but I'm not twelve!" she snapped. "I have friends that care about my safety, I'm sorry if it's not a normal thing for you," she said as she quickly typed away on her phone.

Joanne was impressed with the feisty redhead. No one ever spoke to her like that. She wasn't being rude, she was just standing up for herself, which was admirable.

"I'm sorry, I didn't mean it in a bad way. Go ahead and when you are done, please feel free to join me," Joanne said and took a seat at the table.

She stared as the redhead typed away on her phone. It was clear that she might have her hands full with the feisty redhead and that excited Joanne immensely.

When Alice placed her phone back into her bag, she walked over to the table where Joanne sat waiting. "It's a beautiful place you have here," Alice said.

"Thank you. I enjoy the fruits of my labor. Can I pour you some wine?" Joanne asked as she took the bottle of merlot.

"Yes, please. What do you do for a living?" Alice asked as she lifted the crystal stemware to her lips.

"I'm a businesswoman," Joanne replied. Joanne didn't enjoy this part of the evening. Small talk annoyed her, but it wasn't as if she could just get this woman naked without basic human interaction. "What do you do?" she asked, feigning interest.

"Well, right now I'm in between jobs. My ex left without bothering to leave her half of the rent money and now I have to find something soon or else I'll be evicted."

Joanne was impressed with how Alice didn't seem ashamed or try and hide her current shitty situation.

Joanne couldn't imagine discussing financial hardships with friends, never mind random strangers.

Her private chef prepared a decadent three-course meal, and Joanne enjoyed watching Alice savor every bite. It was obvious that the little redhead wasn't as accustomed to fine dining as she was.

As Alice finished the last of her Crème Brûlée, Joanne poured them another glass of wine. "How about we get comfortable in the hot tub?"

A red flush covered Alice's cheeks. "I, um, I didn't bring any swimwear."

Joanne raised an eyebrow. "Did I ask you to bring swimwear?" she asked as she got up from the table and started to undress as she walked towards the hot tub.

Alice was in obvious shock, but she didn't seem to be the type of girl who would pass up on adventure or opportunity.

Joanne was naked as she stepped into the hot tub aware of the redhead's wide eyes watching her. She sat back in the bubbles and stared at Alice as she started to undress. The skirt Alice wore was now on the floor, and the sight of her standing in only her shirt and pink cotton panties was a huge turn on. Alice removed her shirt revealing that she had no bra on. She had perfect little perky breasts and Joanne enjoyed seeing the shy blush on her cheeks. Her pink nipples were hardening in the night air, begging for attention and their color matched the girl's cheeks.

Alice walked towards the hot tub wearing only her panties. "I'd like you to remove those as well," Joanne said just as Alice was about to get into the hot tub.

Alice took a noticeable big breath and turned her back on Joanne as she slid the panties down her legs.

Joanne felt her pussy tingle at the sight of Alice's perfectly pert little ass. Alice had one of those tiny petite tight little bodies that Joanne always enjoyed. She was exquisite, Joanne thought. To her surprise, Alice's back was covered with a huge tattoo. She made a mental note to ask her about that sometime, but for now she couldn't wait for Alice to get into the water.

As Alice settled into the hot tub, Joanne moved closer and cupped her face. She couldn't wait to taste this woman. She couldn't wait to hear her moan and she couldn't wait to feel her fingers covered in Alice's slickness. "You have a beautiful body. I don't think you should ever cover it up," Joanne whispered just before her lips kissed Alice's waiting mouth.

She could feel sparks between them the moment their lips touched. Alice returned her kisses with a hunger and Joanne could still taste the sugary dessert lingering in her mouth. Joanne's hand cupped Alice's breast and she loved how this woman leaned into her touch.

With her leg strategically placed in between Alice's legs, she felt the redhead start to grind up against her. Changing her tactic, she lifted Alice out of the hot tub, marvelling at her tiny waist in Joanne's hands and sat her on the edge with her legs dangling in the water.

"Open your legs." Joanne commanded firmly and she enjoyed Alice's obedience as her creamy white thighs parted. Her labia was pink and swollen matching her nipples and her cheeks. Her pubic hair was thick red curls trimmed into a neat triangle.

Joanne smiled to herself. *Very nice.*

Joanne moved her gaze to the redhead's green eyes.

"Do you want me to fuck you?" she asked confidently.

The redhead nodded quickly, still blushing endearingly. Joanne smiled again, happy with the way her evening was going.

"I'm going to need you to say the words. Ask for what you want." Joanne held her fingers teasingly close to the redhead's tempting pussy.

"Uh... um..." the redhead mumbled incoherently.

"SAY IT." Joanne knew this one needed a push.

"Um... I'd like you to fuck me.... please..."

"That's better." Joanne smiled sweetly and thrust two fingers inside the redhead feeling her gasp and her body move on entry. She was wet, but still tight. Joanne held her fingers deep inside of the redhead for a minute as she felt Alice's body relax and accept her fingers.

Joanne watched eagerly as Alice's head fell back and she let out a hungry moan. "Your fingers feel so good," she said between ragged breaths.

"This is just the beginning," Joanne teased as she began to fuck Alice with her fingers. This is exactly what she needed after the day she had. Something about fucking beautiful women in her hot tub with the view of her lovely pale body alongside the view of the city at night was just the sweetest release for her. Alice began to really moan and she got wetter and wetter on Joanne's fingers.

This is the life. This is the fucking life.

Just as she could sense that Alice was about to reach orgasm, Joanne withdrew her fingers and used her tongue to give Alice's puffy open labia a long, slow lick. As her tongue reached the clitoris, Alice squirmed but Joanne doubled down. She tasted of sex and chlorine and it wasn't unpleasant. Some of Joanne's best nights had tasted of sex and chlorine.

Holding Alice down, she sucked her clit in and out of her mouth. "I want you to come for me," Joanne said as she increased the suction until Alice couldn't hold back any longer. Alice's moans were almost enough to bring on Joanne's own orgasm. Something about these sweet little submissive women, all it took was a bit of ordering them around and they were putty in her hands. Without warning, she felt Alice's legs clamp down, trapping Joanne's face in between her legs. She screamed and Joanne felt the pulsation of Alice's orgasm in her mouth and against her face.

Mmmmm. Sweet. I'd fuck her again.

When Alice released her grip, Joanne came up for air. She loved the afterglow that was clear on Alice's face. "How about we move this inside?" she said as she helped Alice to her feet.

They walked to Joanne's bedroom, still dripping wet from the hot tub. The plush carpets soaked up most of the water. As soon as they reached her bedroom, the redhead pounced on her. It was clear that she was eager to return the favor; sometimes Joanne let them, sometimes she didn't. Tonight she was in the mood to come in this redhead's mouth.

Alice's mouth clamped down on her nipple and with her free hand, Alice's fingers sought out Joanne's aching pussy.

What tiny hands this redhead has got. Not sure if they will be up to the task. I can barely even feel that.

Joanne felt immediately unsatisfied and frustrated.

"I'll need more of your tiny fingers than that, sweetheart. Let's not mess around here. I'm very turned on. I'd suggest four of your fingers. Fuck me hard with your fingers, find my G spot, and put your mouth on my clit. I want my orgasm now, and I'm not known for my patience."

The redhead looked at her with her big green eyes seeming a little shocked but immediately moving down between her legs and dipping her head to obey.

Joanne felt the girl's fingers pushing inside of her, much firmer and harder this time. She felt them curling upwards, seeking her G spot at the same time she felt the hot wet heat of Alice's mouth on her clitoris.

Mmmm, this is much more like it. She takes feedback well, at least.

Joanne felt the fingers beginning to fuck her. She could hear them moving inside of her wetness and she watched the redhead knelt neatly between her legs face down and pleasuring her and she smiled to herself.

Mmmmm, this is good... but....

Joanne grabbed hold of what she could of Alice's short hair at the back of her head. "Harder." Joanne commanded and after a second's delay, Joanne felt the redhead's fingers moving faster, banging her G spot harder, stretching her open.

She watched as the redhead worked hard to please her, watching her skinny arm as it thrust back and forth quickly and her mouth as it suckled on her clit like a newborn calf. Her eyes were closed in concentration and her long eyelashes flickered.

Joanne could feel her own orgasm building.

Oh... yes..

Oh... fucking... yes...

The hot hot heat flooded right through her body as the waves of her orgasm rushed through her.

Mmmm, this was exactly what I had in mind for tonight.

"You can remove your fingers and mouth now. That was, surprisingly good for someone with such small hands." Joanne said as she relaxed her grip on the redhead's hair.

She felt her sensitive post orgasm pussy twitch as Alice's fingers pulled out of her and she watched as the girl's face came up for air and her big green eyes opened.

Mmm, she looks extra cute with my orgasm all around her mouth.

Joanne pondered going again for a second, but she decided against it as she had some work she needed to finish before her 8am meeting tomorrow. She reached out to the landline on her bedside. 9 was set up for direct dial to her driver.

"I've got a girl I need taking home. She will be down shortly. Her name is..."

Fuck, what is her name? Cute redhead, banging body, tight little pussy?

"My name is Alice," came the voice from next to her, accompanied by an annoyed looking little pixie face.

Fuck, she's really cute when she's mad.

Stop it, Joanne. No time for more fucking tonight. You need to work, then get 8 hours of sleep- your face will start showing your age if you don't get your beauty sleep.

"Alice. Her name is Alice."

"Yes, ma'am. Of course. I'm outside."

"Excellent." Joanne put the phone down.

Joanne watched as the girl looked confused, but took the cue and stretched, getting out of the bed. Her mouth was still damp from Joanne's pussy and Joanne liked that.

She could, of course, have let the girl have a shower but it amused Joanne more to send this girl home dishevelled and smelling of sex.

And, damn, she made dishevelled and just fucked look good.

4

Alice felt in a daze and still smelling of sex as she got in the back of the sleek black Lincoln outside the apartments. She gave the driver her address and took out her phone as he started to drive. She saw that she had twelve missed calls from Max and knew that he was probably going to have another tantrum.

She didn't want the driver to hear about her evening so she sent Max a text from the backseat. *I know it's late. Sorry for not keeping in touch. I'll make up for it over breakfast? Meet me at our Café at 8? Love ya xoxo*

Alice thought back to the craziest evening of her life. That orgasm had been mind-blowing. The ice queen had been like no woman she had ever met in her life. Her pussy was feeling a bit sore but it was definitely worth it for that orgasm. She should be pissed off that the woman was bossy and entitled and kicked her out immediately after sex, but all she could think of was how much she had enjoyed it.

There had been a certain thrill to having been ordered around and then corrected on her technique and told exactly how the woman wanted fucking. And, damn, when she came and exploded in Alice's face. *That* had never happened to Alice before.

When they reached her apartment building, Alice snuck up the stairs again, trying her best to not wake her landlord. The last thing she wanted right now was to deal with him.

Feeling worn out, she undressed and got into bed naked. She set her alarm and drifted off to sleep. Her dreams were filled with hot ice queens ordering her around and telling her off, and when her alarm woke her a few hours later her pussy was aching and wet.

She quickly got into the shower before putting on a pair of yoga pants and oversized shirt. Alice preferred wearing loose clothing. She was blessed with her mother's genes and would turn heads wherever she went from both men and woman. To avoid cat calling and random men trying to pick her up, she usually tried to hide as much of her body as she could, even if it didn't always work.

When she reached the café down the street Max was already waiting. "Where have you been? I've been worried sick," he said with a frown.

"Good morning to you too, Maxie. I know I should have checked in, I'm sorry. I was just kinda lost in the moment," Alice said as she gave him her biggest puppy eyes.

"I'll forgive you if you share all the juicy details," Max said with a wink. Max thrived on moments like these.

"Fine, but can I at least order breakfast first? I'm starving," she asked.

"I already ordered for you, now quit stalling and spill it," Max quickly said.

"Oh, Max, it was amazing, but at the same time, crazy

weird. This woman has a penthouse apartment and we had dinner outside with a stunning view. The food was prepared by her own personal chef and probably the best meal I've had in forever," Alice said.

"Oh my, look who is moving up in this world! Now get to the good stuff," Max interrupted her.

"Well, you were right. She was an absolute bossy bitch. But, um.. .maybe it turns out that is something I like, because, I totally got off on her attitude. And... um.. I'm still *sore!*" she dramatically whispered, wincing as she adjusted herself in her seat.

"Oh my *god. I LOVE IT.* Are you seeing her again?" Max asked, wiggling his eyebrows.

"I don't think so. She was pretty clear about it being a one-time thing. And, well, she couldn't get me out fast enough after we finished." Alice said just as the waitress put down their plates.

Max took a sip of his coffee and said, "As long as you had fun. I told you that you didn't need meaningful connections for great sex."

"Yeah, I know. It kinda sucks, though, because this woman raised the bar for all other woman to come. Where am I going to find another bossy bitch? Like she told me to come for her and my body just did it. Like fucking magic. Like Sophie used to go down on me for hours and sometimes I was just like midway through thinking like I wonder what the weather will be like tomorrow. But, not with this one. She just kept bossing me and pushing me and next thing I'm having the best orgasm of my entire life." Alice said before taking another bite of her pancakes.

"Fucking hell, Alice." He rolled his eyes.

"Alice, good fucks are easier to find than you think. You'll be surprised if you dare to venture," Max retorted.

"This woman has unlocked a whole new sex level in me."

Max laughed.

"I'm glad you had a good time. You needed it. Now that you got that out of your system, what's your plan for the rest of the day?" Max asked.

"I don't know. I suppose I have to look for a new job," Alice said with a sigh.

Max took cash from his wallet to pay for their breakfast and placed it on the table. "Speaking of, I have to get going before I'm late."

"Okay, Maxie. Have a good day," Alice said, sad to see him go.

"Talk to you later," Max said as he gave her a kiss on the top of her head and walked out with a half-eaten muffin in his hand.

Alice finished her pancakes and moved her plate over to make space for her beat up old laptop. She had to find a new job by the end of the day. She opened the browser to search for job vacancies in her area. She replied to a few of the ads but could do nothing more than wait for a phone call for an interview.

Alice packed up to return to her apartment. Just as she was about to place her phone in her bag, a call came through. Alice answered quickly, trying not to sound too eager. Someone just asked her to come in for an interview. Today. She couldn't believe her luck. Usually she would have to wait for days before she got a call.

Alice raced back to her apartment; she only had a little less than two hours to get ready and ensure she made a good impression. Not caring if the landlord heard her enter, she ran up the stairs, two at a time and immediately started the shower again. She felt all sticky and sweaty from running back from the café. Excitement and nerves made Alice move at super speed.

She got in the shower and began practicing the usual interview questions. This was it. This was her chance and she wouldn't mess it up again, she told herself.

JOANNE SAT at her desk and thought of the wonderful night she had with the little redhead. She could still picture her in her too-small skirt and high heels.

What was her name again? Alice. That was it.

Alice had the best body Joanne had ever seen, but it was something else Joanne couldn't get out of her head. That sweet little obedient submissive streak of hers that it looked like she was discovering for the first time last night. Oh, and the way her nipples were the exact same shade of pink as her blushing cheeks and her swollen labia.

Mmmmm.

Even sex with Alice was different than the usual one night stands. Last night, Joanne felt like an animal, her primal urges overruling any sense of restraint and using the redhead's body exactly as she pleased. She could have happily stayed up all night devouring the girl, if she had had the time.

The phone on Joanne's desk returned her to reality. For a moment, she forgot that she didn't have a PA to answer and reluctantly picked up the receiver to take the call. "Yes," she said. It was Kevin saying that he emailed her a few resumes to look at for a personal assistant replacement. "Fine," Joanne said and put the phone down to open her emails.

She scanned the candidates' photos and they were all the normal fresh-faced keen men and women that Kevin usually employed. She didn't think one of them could ever look as good in a tight skirt as Alice did and that's when she had an epiphany.

She remembered Alice telling her last night that she was looking for a job. Desperate for a job to pay her rent in face. The fact that Joanne didn't get involved with her employees didn't matter. Last night was in the past and she rarely ever fucked the same woman twice. Besides, having some serious eye candy around wouldn't do any harm, would it?

Joanne smiled to herself as she took out her phone, brought up the dating app and typed out a message to the redhead.

I have a Personal Assistant position open if you are interested. The pay is very generous. The position is yours on one condition. I personally choose your work clothes of which you will have no say in the matter. If you agree, I will have these outfits delivered to you before you start. Also, please keep in mind, I don't fuck employees. Let me know before close of business if you are interested.

Joanne knew that this was not very professional but she didn't care. The professional route didn't work out for one of her previous assistants. All personal assistants were shit, so at least if the redhead was shit, she would look good and be a pleasant distraction in the office and Joanne would get off on ordering her around. What was the worst that could happen?

She sat back in her chair and fantasized about all the outfits she would have the redhead wear for her and decided to start browsing online for all the provocative items she could find. Seeing no reply on her phone did not discourage Joanne as she always played the long game. She added a few items to her cart in the hopes that Alice would accept her proposal.

FRESH OUT OF THE SHOWER, Alice quickly checked her phone. She had received more messages within the last few minutes. She hopped onto the bathroom counter to read through them before putting on her makeup.

She couldn't believe her luck, she had five interviews lined up and they were all for today. She quickly replied to each invitation by confirming or rescheduling times that clashed and then opened the last unread message. It was from Joanne.

She frowned as she read the text: *I have a Personal Assistant position open if you are interested The pay and benefits are very generous. The position is yours on one condition. I personally choose your work clothes of which you will have no say in the matter. If you agree, I will have these outfits delivered to you before you start. Also, please keep in mind, I don't fuck employees. Let me know before close of business if you are interested.*

Alice was left speechless. "What the actual fuck?" she said to herself. Being a personal assistant would surely pay a lot better than any of the other basic wage positions that she had interviews for, but letting your boss (who gave you the best orgasm of your life the night before) choose your wardrobe, was pervy and kinky. And what would being a personal assistant to a CEO even involve?

Am I ok with that? All of it?

Alice remembered the way Joanne had looked at her in the tight skirt and heels she had worn the night before. Joanne had been undressing her with her eyes the whole evening. She had noticed how Joanne had made her walk to the table in front of her and she had felt Joanne's eyes burning into her ass. Alice remembered how much it had turned her on feeling so desired by someone so attractive and she felt her pussy tingle at the memory.

Does she really just want to watch me in tight clothes? In her office? Is that weird?

She closed the message without replying and quickly got ready for her first interview. Once she was happy with her outfit and makeup, Alice closed her apartment door to leave with time to spare. Just as she was about to exit the apartment building, she noticed the landlord at the mailboxes. Feeling optimistic about the interviews she had today, she greeted him in her chirpiest voice. "Morning! Make sure to check your mailbox on Friday for my rent money," she said with a wink and walked out into the bright, sunny street. She had a good feeling about today and was looking forward to celebrating with Max tonight.

By three o'clock, Alice's morning felt like a distant memory. Her feet had blisters from walking across the city, and it looked like every single interview was unsuccessful. Alice wasn't good in interviews. Her mouth always ran away with her. She always said the wrong thing and then the potential employer always screwed their face up at her like they couldn't believe what she had just said.

For fuck's sake.

Alice sat down on a bench to rest her feet before heading home. That's when she remembered the message she had got from Joanne this morning. She took out her phone to read the message again.

She was beginning to consider Joanne's offer since she was sure to be rejected by every other person she met today. And she needed money for her rent, fast. What was the worst that could happen? So what if she was walking around an office in clothing that someone else chose for her? Wasn't that basically the same as wearing a uniform? So what if she chose high heels and short skirts for her, that was fine, wasn't it?

"Very generous pay and benefits."

Besides, Joanne made it clear that she didn't fuck her employees. So, it wasn't like she was being hired as a prostitute or anything.

Before she could change her mind, Alice quickly replied, *Thank you for the offer. I accept your terms, if you can pay me my first pay check before friday. When would you like me to start?*

Alice saw the three dots on her screen indicating that someone is typing and waited for the text to come through.

You will start tomorrow at 8. Ensure that you are punctual. I don't tolerate lateness. I'll have the driver drop off your new office wardrobe later today. I'll have someone from accounting email you to get your bank account details and I'll ensure you are paid for your first month up front. The office address will be emailed to you also.

Alice refreshed her messages to ensure she didn't miss anything and placed her phone in her bag before starting the long journey home. She had no option but to walk. Her metro card was empty and she didn't have a credit card to reload it. What little cash she had left was at home, and she needed that for a ride to Joanne's office building tomorrow.

As she walked down the streets, she thought about her

life. She knew her biggest downfall was dropping out of college and avoiding the mundane nine-to-five life that so many of her friends were trapped in. Alice could never picture herself as just another cog in the corporate machine of America. Unfortunately, it seemed that she now had no other choice. The blisters on her feet made her walk feel like an eternity, and Alice was relieved when she saw her apartment building come into view.

Upon entering the building, she found her landlord red in the face and shouting at the well-dressed driver who dropped her off after her night with Joanne. He was surrounded by shopping bags and when the landlord noticed her, he turned his attention to her. "This is unacceptable," he said as he waved his chubby arms over the ocean of shopping bags.

"I'm sorry! I will take everything upstairs," Alice quickly said as she grabbed an armful of bags. "This is not your personal depot, you know. One would think that someone who is overdue on their rent wouldn't have money for shopping. Make sure I have your rent on Friday!" the landlord shouted as the driver followed her upstairs with the remaining bags.

Alice quickly unlocked her door and dumped the bags on her futon. She felt embarrassed by the incident with the landlord, but the driver didn't show any indication that he even heard a word. He placed the remaining bags on the floor at the front door and excused himself before walking out and closing the door behind him.

Surrounded by an ocean of shopping bags, she sent Max a text. *You HAVE to come over after work. Make sure you bring wine.*

5

Joanne was waiting in her office impatiently. She looked down at her designer watch and saw that it was only 7:30; she really didn't want to fire the redhead on her first day for coming in late. She spent evening before imagining Alice in the provocative outfits she got for her and couldn't wait to see what she looked like wearing the sexy clothing.

A knock on her door pulled her back to reality. "Yes," she called out. Kevin, the HR manager, stuck his head through the half-open door. "I have a Miss Smith that says you appointed her as your personal assistant?" he asked, confused. Joanne forgot to inform HR about her latest decision, but it didn't matter—she was the CEO after all. If she wanted to employ her own personal assistant she would damn well do it.

"Thank you, Kevin, you can send her through. I'll have her drop by your office later today to finalize her paperwork." Joanne stared at the door waiting for the redhead to make her appearance.

"Good morning, Joanne," the redhead said with a friendly smile as she closed the door behind her.

Joanne was not happy with what she saw. "You will refer to me as Miss Morgan, and what are you wearing?" she asked as she looked the redhead up and down in disgust.

The redhead answered without breaking eye contact. "This was what your driver delivered yesterday. You said I should wear it?"

"I don't believe that the jacket you are wearing was part of my selection," Joanne said as she moved to lean against the front of her desk. She crossed her arms in front of her chest and glared at the redhead.

"Oh, the jacket is mine. The blouse was a bit transparent and I just thought that it would look more professional with the jacket," Alice quickly said.

"I thought I made it clear that you would have no say in the outfits that I selected for you?" Joanne asked with a raised eyebrow, obviously annoyed by Alice not following her instructions.

Alice quickly removed the jacket and draped it over her arm. "You did. It won't happen again," Alice said. She stood up straight with her shoulders back and it was obvious that she was trying her best to bite her tongue.

Joanne took in the woman in front of her. With her beautiful green eyes, Alice didn't have to wear a lot of makeup to look good. The white chiffon blouse clearly showed off the white bra she was wearing as well as Alice's perfect breasts. Joanne wished that she could have her walk around with no underwear but that might be pushing the boundaries. The last thing she needed was a sexual harassment suit.

The pinstripe pencil skirt that she wore hugged her ass perfectly and Joanne didn't regret getting it in a smaller size. With a straight face, Joanne said in a stern voice, "Turn around."

Alice gave a slow turn and presented her back to the CEO. Joanne smiled at the glorious sight in her office.

This is exactly what I want in a PA.

She could feel her own panties growing wet as her mind raced with dirty thoughts. She cleared her throat and walked to take a seat at her huge desk.

"You will find Carol down the hall. She can show you around and take you down to HR to complete your paperwork. Report back when you are done." Joanne said and returned to her desk chair to focus on the large computer screen on her desk. "And, do not wear that fucking jacket ever again."

"Yes, Miss Morgan," she heard Alice say, obediently. She could have sworn she heard some sarcasm in Alice's voice but ignored it for now. She had to try and clear her thoughts before Alice returned with her smoking hot body strutting around in her office again.

AFTER FILLING out what felt like hundreds of different forms in the HR department, Alice grabbed her phone from her bag at her new desk outside of Joanne's office and headed for the Ladies' room. She quickly texted Max.

I swear if I didn't need the money I would be walking out right now. Counting down the hours till I can go home.

It was true. Not only did she despise working in a corporate environment, but Joanne was being a total bitch. She didn't expect preferential treatment, but she at least expected Joanne to be a bit friendlier towards her. The woman knew her intimately after all and had personally chosen her for this job.

After washing her hands, Alice readjusted her too-tight skirt. She could barely walk in the skirt and ridiculously high heels and couldn't blame the other employees openly staring at her. She knew that she was the walking definition of sex on legs but didn't care as long as it meant that she could afford to pay her rent and maybe even buy some groceries.

When she returned to her desk, there was a mousy, skinny guy sitting on her chair. "Miss Morgan wants to see you," he said, not even looking at her.

Alice couldn't believe that she would already be fired and this time she didn't even do anything wrong. She knocked on the door and entered when she heard Joanne's voice from the other side. "You wanted to see me, Miss Morgan?" she said as she waited for Joanne to acknowledge her.

"Yes. I'm sure you noticed your desk is occupied?" Joanne asked as she signed the papers that were cluttering her desk.

"I'm sorry if I did something wrong. I promise I can do better if you give me another chance," Alice quickly said.

"I'm not firing you," Joanne said as she got up from her executive chair. "As my personal assistant, I'll need you close. I can't be calling you every time I need something, so the intern outside will now be my new receptionist."

"Oh, I see," Alice said, confused as to where she would be sitting.

"This will be your new desk," Joanne said as she

pointed towards the ridiculously high stool with a desk top that resembled a tray more than any kind of desk Alice had ever seen in her life.

"You can start by taking down notes for my meeting," Joanne said as she gestured towards the seat and waited for Alice to sit down.

Being close to five foot flat and wearing ridiculous shoes, even if they were Louboutins made it problematic for Alice to get onto the stool elegantly. Her pencil skirt hiked up, making it impossible to cross her legs and cover her underwear, and the chair was set to not only keep her spine straight but to ensure that her breasts were thrust out. Never the less, she wouldn't show Joanne that she was uncomfortable, and once seated, she took out her notepad and pen as she waited for Joanne to continue.

The woman was staring at her with her icy blue eyes. She could feel her gaze moving up and down her legs, and the way that she was smiling was making Alice's pussy tingle. Thrills ran through her body at the memory of what this woman had done to her in the hot tub.

As Joanne started to talk, Alice took down notes. Her gaze was focused on the notepad, but she could feel Joanne's eyes on her body. She subconsciously licked her dry lips.

Alice found her mind drifting back to the hot tub. She had *never* before sat with her legs wide open and her pussy completely exposed and asked someone to fuck her.

I want you to fuck me... please...

She had never had someone just thrust their fingers into her like that with no real warm up. She had been so turned on, sure, and Joanne had just known it would be ok. It had felt like almost too much when the fingers first thrust into her and then as her body adjusted to them, it had felt like the most incredible thing in the world, like the only thing she wanted in the world was Joanne's fingers fucking her, tearing her apart.

Forcing herself to concentrate, Alice reminded herself that Joanne did not fuck her employees. As Joanne finished her monologue, she was standing behind the tall stool that Alice was seated on. She was so close that Alice could feel the heat radiating from her body and her breath in her hair.

Alice felt her heart racing but she didn't dare move. She silently begged Joanne to touch her, but before she could finish her thought Joanne returned to her desk without a word.

Not sure what to do next, Alice closed the notepad and waited for Joanne's next instruction. After a few minutes of uncomfortable silence, Joanne spoke. "I'll have my lunch in my office at twelve. The deli across the road has my standard order. Make sure you have your lunch on the way, I don't want you eating in my office."

Alice was finding it hard to keep quiet. She looked at her watch and saw that Joanne wanted her lunch in 15 minutes, not giving her much time to spare. She excused herself and walked towards the elevator as fast as she could in the restrictive skirt. Her panties were wedged up from the uncomfortable stool, only drawing more attention to her wet pussy. Alice tried her best to ignore it. She had to rush back. She just hoped that the rest of the day would be over soon. This was some kind of exquisite torture.

∽

JOANNE LOOKED at her watch as Alice walked in to her office, carrying a paper bag from the deli. "I told you that I wanted my lunch at twelve, didn't I?" she said, annoyed with Alice's tardiness.

Alice looked at her own watch as she placed Joanne's lunch on her desk. It wasn't even five past twelve yet. "I'm sorry but the owner said they were busier than usual today," she said to Joanne, who was now glaring at her.

"I don't care how busy they are, Miss Smith. I don't have time to waste and I expect you to follow my schedule," Joanne said as she removed her packed smoked chicken salad from the bag.

"No wonder you're having trouble with your personal assistants. In case you haven't noticed, I'm doing my best. The least you could do is say thank you, you know," Alice said as she placed both her hands on her hips.

Joanne was left speechless. She raised an eyebrow. Not once had any of her previous personal assistants dared speak to her like that.

God, how I want to fuck her into submission. Give her something to put in that smart mouth of hers.

"Thank you, Miss Smith. Consider this your first strike," she said to Alice. Joanne could almost see her jaw drop like they show it happen in cartoons. Joanne had to hold back her smile.

It was obvious that Alice was biting her tongue. Joanne was worried that in this case it could be more than just an idiom and Alice might really draw blood. She enjoyed seeing the little redhead all worked up. Apparently, so did her libido.

"Is there anything else I can do for you, Miss Morgan?" Alice asked with an obvious fake smile.

Strip off, bend your hot little body over my desk and beg me to fuck you... Take my strap on in your mouth until you gag... Sit on my face and ride it like a pony...

Stop it, Joanne.

Alice reminded Joanne of a bratty child and her palm itched to give her a well-deserved spanking. That's when Joanne had an idea.

"Do you see the books on the top shelf, Miss Smith?" she asked with a smug smile.

"Yes," Alice answered as she looked at the bookshelf that covered the entire wall from floor to ceiling.

"I need those dusted while I finish my lunch," Joanne said as she kept her eyes on the salad in front of her.

For a moment, she thought that Alice was about to say something but she managed to keep her mouth closed for once and turned around and moved the sliding ladder to the far end of the bookshelf. She turned her back on Joanne, exactly as Joanne wanted.

Fuck, her ass in that skirt. That skirt was an excellent choice. So happy with that.

Every time Alice reached up to remove a book from the top shelf, her skirt would hike up a little further.

The chicken salad in front of Joanne was long forgotten. She couldn't keep her eyes off the redhead whose skirt kept getting shorter and shorter. Joanne moved her chair closer to her desk and slid her hand into her the waistband of her smart black pants and inside her lace underwear. Her pussy was aching with need. She began to rub her fingers lightly over herself, dipping into her wetness and then sliding over her clit.

This is an excellent plan. An orgasm at lunchtime. Mmmm.

She kept her eyes on Alice and her ever increasingly shorter skirt emphasizing her perfect ass. Joanne

Working for the CEO

increased her pace as she watched the redhead and found her silent climax just before Alice turned around.

"Is everything alright, Miss Morgan? Am I doing it right?" she asked.

Feeling flushed from the orgasm and almost being caught, Joanne's tongue was momentarily tied. "Yes. Yes, everything is fine. Please finish up, Miss Smith, I'll be back shortly."

Joanne closed the door of her private bathroom and looked at her rosy cheeks in the mirror. She washed her hands and smiled at her reflection. This redhead might be the best personal assistant she'd ever had. Joanne's mind was working overtime with ideas and fantasies involving Alice, but she had to be careful. Although it might be fun, she couldn't cross the line.

She returned to her desk and pushed her untouched lunch to the side for Alice to discard. She opened her browser on her personal laptop and searched for a few additional items that she thought Alice might need in her new position as her personal assistant.

When Alice was done with the book shelf she asked, "What would you have me assist you with next, Miss Morgan?"

"I need you to prepare the meeting packs for tomorrow. I'm sure Carol showed you the printing room?" Joanne said as she closed her laptop to hide the webpage she had open.

Joanne knew she needed no more distractions for the afternoon so she could get some work done.

"She did. I'll be in the printing room if you need me," Alice said before walking towards the door.

"When you're done you can leave for the day, Miss Smith. My driver will pick you up tomorrow morning at

7:30. Please ensure that you are ready," Joanne said as she opened her laptop again.

"I'll be ready. Thank you, Miss Morgan." Alice walked out leaving Joanne alone with her mischievous shopping list. Joanne couldn't wait for the next day and see just how far she could push her fantasies.

6

Alice uncorked the second bottle of wine and took a seat next to Max. "Are you sure this is a good idea? You know you have to go back to work tomorrow, right?" Max asked.

"Yes, I think it's an excellent idea, Max," Alice said as she filled both their glasses to the rim.

"It's your hangover. Tell me more about this crazy day you had," Max said as he kicked off his shoes to get comfortable.

Alice wasn't sure what to think of her new boss or her new job. Her first day was not what she expected, but for some inexplicable reason she was excited to go back.

"First off, Joanne was a real bitch. Word around the office is that her personal assistants never last long, and if I'm being honest, I'm not surprised," Alice said as she took a sip of her wine.

"And how did you of all people manage not to get fired with such a bitchy boss? Don't get me wrong, you know I love you to bits, it's just that I know how mouthy you can be," Max asked.

Alice gave a little shrug. "Maybe my guardian angel was working overtime today? I never imagined being a personal assistant could be this draining though. And, my feet in these shoes! Oh, god. You would think that shoes this expensive would be comfy at least."

"I'm just happy that you found a way to pay your rent, even if it means you sold your soul to the evil corporate America," Max said as he pulled his face to show disgust.

Alice smiled and said, "I know I said I would never work a normal nine-to-five job but it wasn't all bad, I guess. There is this massive sexual tension with Joanne. She looks at my body like she's a starving woman and I am a banquet, the whole time. It kinda sucks that she has this rule about not having sex with her employees though. That could be an amazing incentive to stick around."

"Yeah, I wouldn't know how that feels. My boss has a stick up his ass and I wouldn't touch his beer belly with a ten-foot pole. If the sexual tension is as thick as you say it is, how do you manage to focus on your job anyways?" Max asked.

"It's not as if I'm doing brain surgery at the office, you know. I'm just there to assist with whatever tasks the boss wants help with," Alice replied.

"You mean like dusting bookshelves? A big corporation like that doesn't employ a cleaning crew?" Max teased her.

Alice emptied her glass and said, "Maxie, as long as it's legal and I'm getting paid, I don't mind if she asks me to swing naked from a chandelier."

The shrill ring from the doorbell interrupted their conversation and Alice raced to the intercom. "Yes?" she said as she pushed the button.

"I have a delivery for Miss Smith," a male voice came

from the speaker.

Confused, Alice replied, "I didn't order anything. You must have the wrong address."

"It's a package from Miss Morgan," the voice said.

Alice wasn't sure what to make of this delivery. "I'll be right down." She quickly put her shoes on and rushed downstairs to get the package. The driver from the other night was waiting at the building entrance, holding a small black box.

She thanked the driver and took the package upstairs to her apartment, curious about its contents. "That doesn't look like work," Max said as she closed the door behind her.

"Yeah, stating the obvious again, huh? I also figured it might be files or something Joanne wanted me to work on," Alice said as she opened the note.

Add this to your wardrobe for tomorrow.

Alice carefully opened the box and once she realized what was inside, she quickly closed it again and put it away in the kitchen drawer.

"What's in the box?" Max asked curiously.

"Oh, uh, it's just my access card," Alice lied.

"Yeah, right. My employers always deliver my access cards to my house, in a box, in the middle of the night," Max replied as he put on his shoes again.

"Whatever, Max," Alice said as she took their glasses to rinse in her kitchen sink.

"I'm calling it a night. Thanks for the wine, hun. Please make sure you lock the door behind me," Max said as he gave Alice a quick hug before walking out the door.

"Talk to you tomorrow, Max, sweet dreams," Alice said as Max walked down the stairs.

Alice locked the door behind Max and quickly pulled

open the kitchen drawer where she stashed the package. She opened the lid, and for a moment all she could do was stare at the contents.

Alice thought that maybe it was some kind of joke, but after the day she had, and assuming that Joanne didn't have a sense of humor, somehow, she knew it couldn't be.

She lifted the butt plug from the box to inspect it closer. It was stainless steel with a sparkly red crystal at the end. Alice was no stranger when it came to sex toys, but to wear one at work? The thought never even crossed her mind before.

Luckily, the plug that Joanne sent her was not too big.

Am I really going to wear this to go to work with? Oh my god, what am I doing? She will be mad if I don't though.

Alice looked at the shiny silver plug in her hand. It looked super expensive and so did the box it came in. She felt an overwhelming desire to obey the request from Joanne. She put it in the bathroom alongside the bottle of lube that came with it, ready to insert before work in the morning.

Once in bed, Alice let her hand drift and she massaged the aching need of her pussy while imagining it was Joanne touching her, and she brought herself to orgasm to release all the pent up frustration of the day.

Giving in to the afterglow of her orgasm, Alice had no problem drifting off to sleep.

JOANNE ARRIVED at the office earlier than usual. She was awake long before her alarm went off. She couldn't wait to see Alice and find out if she followed her instruction. Joanne knew that she was walking on thin ice. She thought that the redhead seemed adventurous enough to wear the gift she sent her; she just hoped that she wasn't wrong.

The view from her office window was spectacular this morning. With clear skies, Joanne could see for miles. She would never grow tired of this view and would usually start her work day by taking it all in. A knock from her office door pulled Joanne back to reality.

"Yes," she said, hoping it was the redhead reporting for duty, but her excitement was instantly replaced by animosity.

"Jo! You look amazing!" It was her ex-wife. This was the last person Joanne wanted to see today. After their divorce, Joanne quickly discovered just how far they grew apart during their marriage and how much both of them changed over the years. The woman standing in her office was far from the woman she met so many years ago.

"What do you want, Layla? I don't remember you having an appointment," Joanne said coldly.

"That's no way to greet the woman that gave up half of her youth for you," the other woman said as she made herself comfortable on the sofa next to the window. As usual, she assumed that she would be welcomed with open arms, but Joanne no longer had any interest or desire to be with her.

"I'm busy, what do you want?" Joanne said, getting straight to the point. She didn't want to give her ex the impression that she actually wanted to spend time conversing with her.

"I just need you to sign these papers," she said as she placed an envelope on the table. "I'm selling the house in Miami and need your signature."

Joanne was annoyed beyond belief. "You could have

just given it to my attorney. I told you numerous times that if you have any queries or need anything you can call my attorney."

"And miss the chance to see you?" Layla replied with a smile. Joanne knew that she came by to drop off the envelope in person to flaunt her new lips. Another procedure paid for with the large alimony she received.

"Layla, I don't have time for this. I'll read through the papers and have my attorney contact yours," Joanne said, trying to get rid of her ex-wife.

At that very moment, the redhead made her appearance. "I'm sorry for interrupting, I'll come back later," Alice said as she started to close the door.

"No, stay," Joanne quickly said. "My guest was just leaving."

Layla grabbed her bag and stormed past Alice, looking her up and down. "Make sure I have those by Monday," she said to Joanne over her shoulder.

Joanne was relieved to be rid of her ex. Now she could give Alice her full attention. She couldn't wait to see the plug that Alice was supposed to be wearing. She locked her office door and turned to face Alice.

She gave Alice a sultry smile and said, "I need you to turn around, bend over and raise your skirt up for me."

Joanne watched as Alice's eyes widened in shock. Joanne enjoyed shocking her.

I wish I had seen her face when she opened the box.

Timidly, and glancing between the blinds on the windows separating Joanne's office from the rest of the employees and the big glass panes opening out onto the whole city, Alice turned slowly around and bent forward awkwardly hitching her tight skirt up. Her legs looked incredible in the black Manolo Blahniks. Joanne noticed her face turning a pretty pink. Joanne noticed the white lace panties as the skirt reached above Alice's ass. "My dear Alice, how am I supposed to see what you know I want to see with those pretty little panties on?" she asked teasingly.

Slowly, Alice pulled down the panties, which made Joanne's heart race. She was so turned on by the sight in front of her and wished she could fill Alice's pussy with her fingers while she was wearing the plug. She could imagine Alice's moans. She still thought about the appreciative sounds Alice made while she was being fucked.

Joanne had Alice stand bent over like that for a few minutes with her panties just above her knees and the red gemstone glinting in place of where her asshole was.

Alice was wearing the buttplug as instructed and the very thought of it ran thrills through Joanne. It was the most beautiful sight she had seen in a very long time. The cheeks of Alice's ass were full and round in this position.

I have to fuck her from behind one day.

Stop it. No fucking employees, remember?

"You'll need to re-lube at regular intervals through the day. Don't get sore."

Alice nodded and murmured agreement.

Joanne walked to her desk to take a seat. "You are such a good girl, Alice," she said with a satisfied smile. "Get me a latte from downstairs and then we can go over this week's schedule."

Without a word, Alice pulled up her panties and fixed her skirt. She seemed to be more than a little flustered when she closed the door behind her and Joanne knew that the redhead was just as turned on as she was.

She had to find release before Alice returned or she wouldn't be able to think straight. She took her trusted bullet vibrator from her bag and held the toy to her aching clit. She closed her eyes and thought back to the night that Alice came over to her apartment. She remembered how good Alice tasted and how good it felt when Alice fucked her. Joanne came hard and it took a moment for her to catch her breath.

Joanne was starting to regret her No Fucking Employees rule.

What a stupid fucking rule.

She knew the release she felt was only temporary and that it was going to be a long day for her with Alice working so close to her.

It only took a few minutes for Alice to return with her coffee. "Thank you," Joanne said as Alice placed the cup on her desk.

"You're welcome," Alice said, clearly surprised by Joanne remembering to say thank you. "Would you like to get started on your appointment schedule for next week, Miss Morgan?" she asked.

"Yes, you can take a seat at your desk," Joanne said. She took a sip of her coffee as she watched Alice struggling to get onto her high stool with the plug. The skirt she was wearing today was shorter and tighter than the previous day making it completely impossible for Alice to cover up the view Joanne had of her panties.

Joanne sat back in her chair taking in the sexy view she had in front of her. She could feel her own pussy growing wet again. She wished she could have Alice on her knees at her desk relieving her of all the pent-up frustration, but since she couldn't break her own rules, she would have to embrace this tension between them.

"Let's get started, shall we?" Joanne said before she could get lost in thought again.

7

Alice woke up after a quiet night at home alone. She felt a kind of relief when Max said that he wouldn't be able to come over; she needed some alone time. It wasn't that she was physically tired or mentally drained. She was aroused like never before and it wasn't only because of the plug Joanne had her wear the previous morning. It was the way Joanne looked at her, the way she made her feel. There was a fierce sexual tension between them that was driving Alice crazy. She was craving this woman like she never craved anyone before.

Just as Alice was about to get into the shower and get ready for work, she received a text. It was from Joanne. *There is a package at your door. Make sure you wear it with the blue dress today.*

Quickly, Alice opened her door and reached for the gift bag before any of her neighbors could see her. She removed the item, which she could only describe as a lacy string. Alice laid out the stringy item on her unmade bed and realized that it was, in fact, a pair of crotchless panties. She knew the lingerie store that it was purchased at and was sure that this little piece of fabric probably cost more than what she used to make in a week.

As Alice got her shower started, she took the blue dress out of her closet. She was trying to avoid wearing this one as it was the shortest of all the dresses that Joanne bought her. Alice was no prude but she wasn't use to drawing so much attention to herself. Usually, she would do the opposite and try to hide as much of her body as she could, but she liked the feeling she got when Joanne looked at her in the sexy outfits.

Standing in the shower, underneath the hot spray of water, Alice lathered up her body with her aromatic bodywash. Her nipples ached for attention as she cupped her breasts. She imagined it was Joanne's fingers pinching her nipples and she let out a small moan. Moving her one hand to her tingling sex she started to rub her clit with slow sensual movements, trying to drag out her orgasm for as long as possible.

The ringing of her doorbell caught her off guard, and wrapping a towel around her body, Alice quickly ran to the intercom. "Yes," she said a little out of breath.

"I'm sorry to bother you, Miss, but we need to leave in order to avoid you getting to the office late," the driver's voice said from the little speaker box.

"I'll be right down, thank you," Alice said before dashing back to the shower to rinse off the suds. She was scolding herself for losing track of time. The last thing she wanted was to disappoint Joanne.

Alice got dressed in record time and grabbed her makeup bag so she could do her makeup in the car on her way to the office. When she reached the driver holding open the car door she quickly got in, knowing that the

Working for the CEO

strangers on the street must have caught a glimpse of her crotchless panties but she didn't care. All Alice cared about at that moment was to reach the office on time.

Luckily, the traffic on her way to work wasn't too bad and she was thankful that the driver was making an effort to get her to work as fast as possible. She got into the elevator and checked her watch. Alice saw that she was ten minutes late and hoped that maybe Joanne wouldn't notice.

Alice softly knocked on Joanne's office door. She let out the breath she was holding when she got no reply and slowly opened the door. Joanne was nowhere to be seen and Alice walked towards her seat to get ready for the day.

"That's strike two," Joanne's voice suddenly said behind her. A cold shiver ran down Alice's spine and made the hair on her arms stand up. Alice had no idea where Joanne came from.

"I'm sorry for being late but it's only a few minutes," she quickly said as she turned around to face the gorgeous icy blonde with the piercing blue eyes.

"Alice, you need to understand that time is money and I don't like wasting either," Joanne said as her eyes travelled up and down Alice's body obviously liking what she was seeing.

"You know that sometimes life happens, right?" Alice said without thinking.

Clearly caught off guard by Alice's unwarranted remark, Joanne moved closer. She was standing so close that Alice could feel heat radiate from her body again. Every nerve in her body was calling out to Joanne to touch her, silently praying to feel her hands on her skin. Not being able to finish herself off in the shower was making her lusting pussy ache more than other days in the office.

Joanne just smiled, making Alice wonder if this woman knew what she was feeling. "Have a seat," Joanne said as she folded her arms across her chest and waited for Alice to get onto her stool. From experience Alice knew that getting onto the too-high seat in the too-short dress would expose her newest gift from Joanne in full view. Alice didn't even bother to get on to the chair in a modest manner and when she saw the smile on Joanne's face, she knew that giving Joanne a full view of her pussy framed by the sexy lace was working in her favor.

"I love the way you wear my gift," Joanne said as she gave Alice a wink. "I think going forward that should be the only underwear you wear to the office. I'll have to call the store for a few more of those."

Alice was left speechless, which was unusual for her. "Thank you?" she managed to get out as she felt her heart racing at the thought of getting her stool soaked by her arousal.

"As a matter of fact, I have an appointment in a few minutes. I'll call ahead and while I'm busy, you can go pick up the new items for your wardrobe," Joanne said and took out her phone to make the call.

Alice stared at the Joanne as she spoke to the lingerie store manager on the phone to order one of the lacy strings in every available color. "The store manager is expecting you," Joanne said. "Unfortunately, my driver is not available but since it's only a few blocks I'm sure walking won't be an issue."

"I can't walk the streets wearing this," Alice said as she gestured to her short skirt. She didn't mind wearing the outfits for Joanne but walking around in the streets with a dress that barely covered her exposed pussy was not something that Alice wanted to do.

"Alice, when you are on my time you will do as instructed. It's barely even a couple of blocks. I'll be done with my meeting in half an hour. Make sure that you're not late again." Joanne said as turned around to walk to her desk.

Swallowing her pride, Alice got up from her stool and walked towards the door. She didn't understand why she felt turned on by Joanne's instruction, but she didn't have time to think about that as she didn't want to be late again.

She walked to the store and back as fast as her high heels and short skirt allowed her, constantly checking her watch to avoid being late. Alice pressed the button for the elevator and saw the out of order sign. Glancing at her watch again, she already knew that taking the stairs would mean that she was not going to be back in Joanne's office in time.

With no other choice, Alice opened the door to the stairway and started her climb as fast as she could. She silently prayed that Joanne would still be in her meeting.

JOANNE LEANED AGAINST HER DESK, waiting for the redhead to return. She smiled to herself as she thought of how she sabotaged the poor woman. She knew that having the out of order signs put up at the elevators would result in Alice being late, and she was looking for any excuse to get her hands on the sexy redhead.

A soft knock on her office door announced Alice's arrival. "Strike three," Joanne said as Alice walked in and closed the door behind her.

"The elevator is out of order. I tried to get back as fast

as I could," Alice quickly defended herself. Obviously, she thought that three strikes meant that she would be fired.

"I don't tolerate excuses," Joanne said as she moved towards Alice. It was obvious that the stubborn redhead was fuming inside. She took the shopping bags from Alice and placed them against the wall. "Walk towards my desk and face the wall," she calmly said.

Alice gave her a suspicious glance but walked towards her desk anyways. Joanne could see that Alice was trying her best to hold her tongue. "Bend down and place both palms flat on the desk," Joanne instructed her.

Joanne was extremely turned on by the woman bending over her desk. The too-short skirt exposed her perfect ass and the high heels emphasized her sexy legs with gorgeous calves. "Spread your legs wider," Joanne said as she walked closer to the bent-over woman.

She could see Alice's slickness glistening on her inner thigh and although she seemed uncomfortable and unsure of her current situation, Joanne knew that Alice was just as turned on as she was. Joanne hiked up Alice's dress to expose her full backside.

With one hand on Alice's lower back, she used the other to slowly caress the soft skin of her ass cheeks, and just as Alice leaned into her touch, her palm came down hard on her right ass cheek, making the redhead jump.

"Stay still, Alice. That is only the first one. You will take ten and not make a sound or move," Joanne instructed as she looked at the red handprint on Alice's ass cheek. "Do you understand, Alice?" she asked.

"Yes, I understand," Alice said as she tried to catch her breath.

"This time, I'll even count them out for you," Joanne said as she prepared herself for the next slap and without another word her hand came down hard on Alice's unblemished ass cheek. "Two," Joanne said as she admired her hand prints on Alice's ass.

She waited for Alice to relax again before continuing, dragging out the suspense. She did this until she reached ten. Alice was breathing hard, and before realizing what she was doing, Joanne's fingers dragged through the redhead's soaking slit.

Alice gasped and moaned and involuntarily her body leaned into Joanne's hand, but Joanne had other plans. She turned the redhead to face her and made a show out of licking Alice's juices from her fingers.

"You start with a clean slate on one condition, Alice," Joanne said as she stared into Alice's green eyes. "You are no longer allowed to touch yourself or come unless I tell you to, is that clear?"

Clearly confused and still in a haze from the spanking, all Alice could manage was to nod her head in agreement.

"Now, go clean yourself up, we have a lot of work to do," Joanne instructed before walking to her private bathroom in search of her own release.

8

Joanne was frustrated like never before. Her mind was occupied with thoughts of Alice no matter what she did. She knew that it was her own fault for teasing the redhead the way she did and for her own stupid rule of not fucking her employees, but no matter how many times Joanne tried to get rid of her frustrations through masturbation, she just couldn't quite find the release she craved.

It had been two weeks since Alice started as her personal assistant, and although Joanne planned to abide by her rule of not fucking employees, she could hardly say she was keeping it professional and it was getting harder and harder to push her desires aside. The sexual tension between them was unlike anything Joanne ever felt, and deep down she knew that there was only one way she could satisfy her hunger.

Not being the type of woman to break her own rules, Joanne wondered if maybe it would be better if she transferred Alice to a different department. Alice might be the most adequate assistant she ever had but her sexy feistiness and the sexual tension between them was becoming a distraction that Joanne was seriously struggling to ignore.

The moment Joanne walked into her office, she realized she could never get rid of Alice. There she was; Alice was standing with her arms crossed over her chest, staring down her ex who was making herself comfortable in her office.

"Jo, please tell this silly girl to stop watching me like I'm about to steal something from your office," her ex said when she walked in.

"Morning, Miss Morgan. Your guest didn't have an appointment so I thought I'd stay here until you arrived," Alice quickly said without taking her eyes off of her ex.

At that very moment Joanne's heart swelled with pride. It seemed as if Alice might be a little protective over her. "Thank you, Alice," Joanne said.

Layla got up from her seat and stood in front of Joanne. "I'm waiting on the papers you were supposed to sign," she said.

Not fazed by her ex-wife's intimidation tactics, Joanne calmly walked over to her desk and removed the manila envelope from her top drawer. "As I previously said, I would prefer if you would work through my attorney."

Joanne held out the envelope to her ex-wife. "There's your paperwork. No please go. I have a busy day."

Her ex snatched the envelope out of her hand. "You should get a leash for your little watchdog, shouldn't she be at school, anyway?" she said as she gave Alice a look of disgust.

Layla's insult pushed Joanne's buttons and she was now fuming. "Get out *now!*" she said to her ex through clenched teeth. Layla stormed out of the office and slammed the door behind her.

"Is there a reason why I don't have my coffee waiting on my desk?" she asked Alice.

"As a matter of fact there is, or did you miss the part where I was waiting for you to handle your ex-wife?" Alice said with her voice raised a little.

"I didn't ask you to do that, did I?" Joanne fired back.

"No, you didn't but the least you could do is say thank you and stop being such a bitch to me," Alice said.

"If I'm a bitch it's because woman like yo—" and Alice cut her off by kissing Joanne passionately. Joanne's predatory hunger returned and she eagerly returned the kiss with fierceness.

Alice broke their kiss and took a step back leaving both women staring at each other in ragged breath. Joanne took a seat at her desk and pulled Alice down on her knees pushing her beneath the desk. "You better not start something you can't finish," she said, hitching her skirt up and pulling her own panties to the side and Alice hungrily went to work.

There was no teasing or slow sensual licks. Alice was devouring her like a starved animal and Joanne could feel her orgasm approaching fast. She pulled Alice's head closer to her soaking pussy and just as she was about to start grinding against her hungry mouth, she heard a knock on the door.

Quickly, she pulled down her skirt to cover herself as Alice hid underneath her desk. Without waiting for a reply Kevin peaked around the door. "Someone said they heard loud voices coming from your office. Is everything okay? Do you need me to call security?" he asked as he scanned her office.

"If I need security, I will call them myself, Kevin. Everything is fine," Joanne quickly said as she tried her best to keep her voice steady.

"Of course. I'm sorry for barging in," Kevin said as he closed the door behind him.

Joanne pushed back her desk chair and stared at the tiny redhead who was covering her mouth to smother her giggle. "Not funny," Joanne said as she held out her hand to help Alice up.

"Alice. This is bad for business, I really need to do some work," Joanne sighed.

"But..." Alice tried to protest.

"Why don't you take the rest of the day off and when you return on Monday, we can just pretend that this never happened," Joanne said.

Clearly not happy with being sent home, Alice quickly grabbed her things from her desk. "I'll see you on Monday then," she said as she walked out.

Joanne knew that she handled the situation wrong, but she couldn't let sex get in the way of her work. She sat down at her desk, even more frustrated than before and tried to think of how to fix things.

ALICE COULDN'T BELIEVE that Joanne sent her home. The moment they shared was amazing. It happened spontaneously and it felt so right. Maybe it only felt so intense because of all the tension that was building between the two of them over the past two weeks. It still didn't change the fact that Joanne didn't want her around the office for the rest of the day.

Since Alice got home a couple of hours ago, she'd

been pacing her apartment up and down trying to clear her head. She was counting down the hours so she could meet up with Max and vent about her day. Unfortunately, he had to work late and it would still be a couple of hours that she would have to try and keep busy.

Alice opened her laptop to watch a movie to distract her from thoughts of Joanne. She dozed off halfway through the movie only to be woken by phone vibrating next to her. Alice reached to her bedside table and saw Joanne's name on the screen. She wasn't sure what to think as Joanne never called her after hours.

Cautiously, Alice answered, "Hello?"

The line was quiet for a moment and then Joanne said, "Hi Alice. I'm sorry to bother you at home after working hours but I need a favor from you."

"Seriously? After sending me home today, you're asking me for a favor?" Alice couldn't believe the audacity that Joanne had.

"Listen, I'm sorry I sent you home. I crossed a line with you today, I broke my own rules and in the moment, I just thought that it was the right thing to do," Joanne apologized. "We can discuss the matter in person when you come over, if you want."

"Fine. What's the favor?" Alice asked.

"I forgot a couple of files on my desk and I need them to work from home this weekend; I would send the driver but he is running other errands for me. Could you please pick up the files and bring them to my penthouse?" Joanne asked.

"You need your files tonight? You need your files on a Friday night? Don't you have a life?" The words came out before Alice realized what she said. "I'm sorry, I didn't mean it like that. I'll drop the files off in the next hour."

"Thank you, Alice, if you check my second drawer you will find a set of house keys. You can just let yourself in when you get here. Get a cab from HQ cabs and charge it to my personal account- I've pre-authorized it. I'll be on the deck."

Joanne disconnected and Alice looked at the phone in her hand. She really didn't feel like getting dressed to go all the way to the other side of town to drop work files, but since Max wouldn't be available for a few hours she might as well stay busy.

Alice called HQ cabs and ordered a cab on Joanne's account for 5 minutes time. She quickly got dressed. When they reached the office building, she asked the driver to wait while she quickly ran inside to get the files. She grabbed the files, and on her way out remembered the house keys. When Alice was sure she had everything, she got back into the waiting vehicle and tried to relax as the driver drove to Joanne's address.

It was only a couple of minutes away from the office and soon Alice was unlocking the front door to Joanne's penthouse where she had only been once before on that first incredible night. She placed the files on the table in the foyer and went in search of Joanne. "Hello?" she called out as she approached the deck.

"Hi Alice, thanks so much for bringing me my files," Joanne said. "Why don't you join me for a glass of wine?" Joanne was wearing only a silk kimono that was loosely tied at the waist and Alice thought it looked like she had no underwear on. She could see her nipples through it.

For a moment Alice thought she might be dreaming, that maybe she didn't wake up from her nap like she thought. Joanne was being the complete opposite from this morning when she sent her away. "I don't want to intrude," Alice said.

"You're not, there is something I'd like to discuss with you, please?" Joanne said as she gestured towards the outdoor seating at the fireplace.

Alice found Joanne's behavior very strange but took a seat as she was curious about what she wanted to discuss. She took a sip of the merlot that Joanne offered her and sat back waiting to hear what Joanne had to say.

"As you might know by now, I find you incredibly sexy, like no-one I've ever met before." Joanne started out. Her blatant honesty almost caused Alice to spit out her wine.

"I'm not sure what to say," Alice replied, still in shock from Joanne's confession.

"I think that you also feel the sexual tension between us, am I correct?" Joanne asked.

"You're not wrong," Alice said as she took another sip of her wine.

"I have a proposal. Since you seem to be the adventurous type, how would you feel about a mutual beneficial arrangement with no strings attached?" Joanne asked.

"You mean, fuck buddies?" Alice asked.

"If you want to put it in a cruder way, yes," Joanne said as she put her glass of wine on the table before placing her hand on Alice's leg. "Would you be able to enjoy my company without any expectations?"

Alice thought back to their first encounter after Joanne found her on the dating app. It was actually easier to just have fun with someone and not having to worry about making a good impression or creating any expectations. "If there are no expectations from either side, I'm in."

"Well, I do have one small expectation," Joanne said.

Alice rolled her eyes. "I guess I should have known."

"You should know that I don't do sleepovers. There will be no spending the night together. Are you okay with that?" Joanne asked.

Alice thought back to the first time she visited Joanne at her penthouse and how she was evicted the moment Joanne had come. She felt a little relieved knowing that it was a normal thing for Joanne and that she didn't do anything wrong that night. "Yeah, I suppose that's fine with me," Alice said.

"You'll need to sign this agreement for the HR department which says you consent to a sexual relationship with me in and out of the office and you forego any right to bring any sexual harassment suits against me." Joanne thrust a document and a pen into Alice's hand. Alice gave it a cursory glance, but she didn't care about signing her rights away. She needed so badly to for Joanne to fuck her that she would have signed anything. She signed on the dotted line and handed the paper back to Joanne who placed it down on the ornate table with her wine and sat down on the sofa.

"Well, in that case," Joanne said as she laid back on the sofa and opened her legs, "Why don't you finish what you started this morning."

Alice felt her heart race at how unashamed Joanne was. The sexual energy between them was crazy. She took another sip of her merlot and knelt down making herself comfortable in front of Joanne's crotch. This was different from earlier this morning. There was no need to rush things.

She kissed her way along Joanne's inner thigh to her waiting pussy. A long, slow lick through Joanne's slit made Joanne moan. More long slow licks, Alice knew she would never get tired of the taste of her, never get tired of pleasing her, never get tired of being on her knees for her. Alice pushed her tongue inside Joanne and enjoyed the moan that came with it. Alice looked up briefly and saw Joanne's eyes fixed on her watching every move she made. Her lovely blue eyes were glazed with desire.

Alice moved her fingers to Joanne's wetness remembering exactly what Joanne had told her to do last time. Four fingers. G spot. Hard.

Alice started with three fingers, Joanne was so wet and wanting, she quickly added a fourth and then her thumb with her mouth on Joanne's clitoris.

Alice felt Joanne opening right up for her and a quick thought entered her head.

Fisting.

She wanted to give Joanne exactly what she wanted. Should she ask first? Should she just do it? Is that what she wanted?

Joanne's pussy seemed to be pulling her hand in as Alice thrust into her.

Joanne grabbed hold of her hair and tried to pull her head closer to her pussy, but Alice had other plans. With her fingers still deep inside Joanne's pussy, Alice loosened the kimono and moved her mouth to Joanne's breast. She sucked her nipple deep into her mouth knowing Joanne was watching her.

"Fuck, that feels so good," Joanne's words were stilted and between moans. She was lost in the feeling.

Alice pushed her whole hand inside Joanne's slippery wetness, curling her fingers round into a fist, preparing herself to get told off. There was no telling off, just Joanne's legs opening wider, Joanne's head tipping back exposing her long pale throat, Joanne screaming as she orgasmed hard, tensing around Alice's hand, almost crushing it. Alice could feel electricity from Joanne's pussy pulsing through her hand. It was the most incredible feeling in the world. She relaxed her mouth on Joanne's nipple and rested her hand which was still deep inside Joanne.

She didn't dare move until she was told to.

Joanne came to and looked down at Alice with her nipple still in her mouth.

"You sweet, sweet girl, that was amazing. Keep your hand inside of me and kiss me."

Alice moved her mouth up from Joanne's nipple and crooked her wrist so she could try and reach. It was awkward and hard but as her lips met Joanne's and her tongue pushed inside Joanne's mouth, Joanne's pussy clamped down again on her hand. Another orgasm. Alice smiled into Joanne's moans.

"I want you to slide your hand out of me very slowly." Joanne was back.

Alice gently unfurled her fingers and slowly and very carefully slid out of Joanne. It wasn't Alice's first time fisting someone and she was very aware of how intense it could be for the receiver.

Joanne pulled Alice closer and kissed her fiercely. Joanne pushed her leg up into Alice's crotch and Alice grinded her soaking pussy in search of her own climax, but it seemed that Joanne had other plans.

She led Alice to her bedroom and had her lie down on the huge, four-post bed. "I need to know if you trust me, Alice," Joanne whispered in her ear between kisses.

"I suppose," was all Alice could say in her confusion.

"I'd like to try something," Joanne continued. "If you

feel uncomfortable and you want me to stop what I'm doing, I want you to say the word *red*."

"And if I don't?" Alice asked curiously.

"If you don't want me to stop, I won't. Now, undress," Joanne said with a cheeky smile as she got up from the bed and walked over to the chest of drawers against the wall.

Joanne returned with silk scarves and as she looked down at Alice lying on her back she asked, "Are you ready, Alice?"

Alice could only nod her head, excited about what Joanne was about to do.

Expertly, Joanne tied her spread eagle to the bed before using the final scarf to blindfold her. Alice found herself in total darkness, and being robbed of her sense of sight made her entire body feel extra sensitive.

Alice felt Joanne stroke her breasts with something soft and fluffy. The sensation made Alice arch her back craving more. The soft strokes were followed by sensual licks from Joanne's tongue. "I need more," Alice said.

"We have all night, Alice," Joanne said as the stroking moved down to Alice's inner thighs.

It felt like Alice's clit was about to explode. She felt Joanne's warm breath on her exposed pussy and tried to move her aching sex closer to Joanne's mouth.

Her eagerness only made Joanne tease her more. She kissed Alice's labia before moving her mouth away from her pussy and back up to her neck.

Joanne placed her leg in between Alice's and began to move in a slow rhythm. "Please, I need more," Alice begged, but instead of increasing pressure or speeding up, Joanne moved away.

Surrounded by darkness, Alice was momentarily

worried that Joanne was just going to leave her there, worked up and helpless; but then she felt Joanne kneeling over her head and then leaning forwards over her body. She could smell the sweet scent of Joanne's arousal as she hovered above her head and when Joanne's mouth clamped down on Alice's pussy, Alice began to feed on Joanne's sex.

"Don't come yet," she heard Joanne say. Being so close to the edge and having to hold back her orgasm was torture. Alice used her mouth to try and get Joanne off again as fast as she could, so she could find her own release before she exploded.

"I'm so close," Alice's voice was muffled by Joanne's pussy. Alice was unsure of how much longer she could hold it in.

The suction on her clit intensified as Joanne pushed her fingers into her soaked pussy. "Come for me, Alice, now." Joanne said and returned to sucking her aching clitoris. Alice felt Joanne beginning to grind her own pussy against Alice's face. She could barely breathe as her own orgasm tore through her, ever obedient to Joanne's command, fiercer than ever before, smothered by Joanne's sex. Seconds later, just as Alice thought she might suffocate, Joanne orgasmed, gushing all over Alice's face and in her mouth.

Alice swallowed fast and gasped in air as Joanne lifted away from her. Her arms and legs were still bound.

That had for sure been the most explosive sex of her life. Nothing compared to that. All of it.

Fuck.

Joanne moved to lay down next to Alice and removed her blindfold, causing Alice to shut her eyes against the sudden light.

"That was fucking amazing," Alice said.

Joanne smiled and said, "You are fucking amazing."

After a few minutes of basking in the afterglow, Joanne gently untied Alice. "Can I get you something to drink?" she asked.

"Some water would be great, thank you," Alice said as she sat up in Joanne's bed.

Joanne returned with two bottles of water. She smiled down at Alice as she handed her one of the bottles. "Thank you for coming over tonight."

"No, thank *you* for giving me the orgasm of my life," Alice quickly replied with a witty pun.

Joanne rolled her eyes as she took a seat next to Alice. "You're welcome to have a shower before the driver takes you home."

Alice momentarily forgot that she was expected to leave. She knew that she agreed to Joanne's no-staying-over rule but didn't expect to leave right after sex. Again. Especially since her legs was still feeling a bit unsteady. "It's fine. I'll shower when I get home," she said as she got up and started to look for her clothes.

"Alice, are you sure that you are okay with this agreement?" Joanne asked as she watched Alice getting dressed.

"Yeah, of course I'm sure," Alice quickly said, avoiding eye contact.

"Good. I'm glad you are happy with our arrangement," Joanne said. "I'm looking forward to doing this again soon."

There was an awkward silence that filled the room. "I guess I'll just get an Uber then," Alice said as she took out her phone.

"Don't be silly. My driver will take you home," Joanne

said as she walked over to the intercom to arrange Alice's transportation.

Alice did a quick scan of the room to ensure she had all her things. "Guess that's it then?" she asked Joanne.

Joanne gave her a soft, sensual kiss and walked her to the foyer where the driver was already waiting. "Have a good night, Alice," she said.

Alice turned around and followed the driver to the black Lincoln. Alice made herself comfortable in the backseat and almost drifted off to sleep before they stopped at her apartment complex.

After thanking the driver, Alice walked upstairs to her apartment and fell down on her bed. She stared at her ceiling replaying the events of the evening. Alice still couldn't wrap her head around her agreement to Joanne's request. When she woke up that morning, it was the last thing she imagined would happen.

Why was sex with her boss the most mindblowingly incredible thing to ever happen to her?

9

Joanne woke up feeling refreshed. The tenderness between her legs brought a smile to her face as the memories of the sexy little redhead tied to her bed filled her thoughts. It was an evening she would be, hopefully, repeating soon and repeating regularly. She loved how trusting Alice was when she bound her to her bed and how she responded to her every touch.

Fresh from her morning shower, Joanne took a seat at the breakfast table to read through her work emails. After opening and reading the fifth email and realizing that she had no idea what she just read, Joanne walked over to the balcony to take in the view from her deck.

It was a crisp autumn day and Joanne found the breeze refreshing. Joanne was glad that she decided to break her own rule about not fucking employees. After all the torture she put herself through with Alice's sexy body taunting her in the office daily, the choice to break her own rule was easy to make.

Joanne was wondering what Alice was doing right at that moment and decided to send her a text to check in.

Good morning gorgeous. How are you today?

She hit send and sat back down at the table to finish her juice. Her phone vibrated on the table and she unlocked the screen to read Alice's reply.

Morning. Just woke up. Thanks for last night. I slept like a baby.

Joanne smiled down at her phone knowing exactly what Alice meant. She couldn't remember the last time she slept so well. She knew that she wanted to see Alice again. Although last night took care of all her immediate frustrations, her body was lusting after the sexy redhead.

Would you be interested in a repeat of last night? I'm free today.

It felt strange to say that she was free. Usually by now she would have been working for a few hours already. She avoided the files Alice left behind on purpose since she didn't want anything to ruin her mood.

I already have plans. Maybe we can meet up later?

Joanne should have known better than to expect someone like Alice to just lounge around in her apartment all weekend. She quickly typed a reply.

Sure. Send me a text if you'd like to meet up. Have a good day.

Joanne found herself in unfamiliar territory. She wasn't in the mood to dive into work and honestly didn't know how to keep busy. She decided that she might as well take the day to pamper herself and she called to schedule a couple of treatments at her favorite spa.

Joanne got dressed and for the first time in a long time she got into the backseat of her Town Car and took in the sights of the city as the driver took her to her scheduled appointments. Joanne couldn't keep her thoughts from drifting back to the sexy redhead, and she knew that it was going to be a long day as she waited to hear back from her. She didn't want to get her hopes up, but she was being honest with herself and hoping that she could see her again tonight.

"You did *what*?!" Max said so loud that the entire yoga studio turned around to shush them.

"God, Max, keep it down, will you?" Alice quickly said as she stretched in the next pose.

"You can't drop a bomb like that and expect me to be all Zen," Max said next to her.

"Let's talk after our session, okay?" Alice asked.

"Fine, but with your fancy new job it's your turn to pay for our smoothies," Max said.

Alice loved that Max was always so enthusiastic about her ventures. To most people he seemed like a stereotypical, overdramatic queen, but Alice knew the real Max just like he was the only person in the entire world that knew the real her.

After their yoga session, Alice paid for their smoothies as promised- as promised her new salary was *very* generous- and they made themselves comfortable on the green grass of the park. It was a nice day to be outside, and Alice wondered if Joanne ever allowed herself some free time to enjoy simple moments like these.

"Earth to Alice..." Max said while waving a hand in front of her face.

"I'm sorry, I must have spaced out," Alice said before taking another sip of her strawberry smoothie.

"No shit, Sherlock," Max teased her. "Now, tell me

everything." Max made himself comfortable sitting cross legged next to her on the grass.

Alice gave a small shrug. "There's not really much more to tell you, Max."

"You're such a liar. So let me see if I understand your current situation. Basically you signed a legal document agreeing to have your brains fucked out by your super hot boss whenever it suits her? So long as you go home straight afterwards? That seems a bit cold and anti-climactic, but I guess that is what a no-strings arrangement would mean," Max said.

"It's not like you really stick around after your one-night stands, Max," Alice said.

"Yeah, I know. I suppose I was just secretly hoping that this might be your happily ever after. You know, sort of a rags to riches, Cinderella ending," Max said with enthusiastic gestures.

Alice knew better than to entertain any idea of what Max just said. "Well, Max, if I'm honest, I am happy. This arrangement will work for me, and if by some miracle I meet someone else that could potentially be my life partner, I'll just break it off."

Max looked at her with concerned eyes. "Alice, just be careful, okay? I do not want to see you get hurt again."

"Don't worry, Max, this is different. With Joanne I know from the beginning that it's just for fun," Alice said.

"Speaking of fun, why don't we go out tonight? I heard they are hosting karaoke night at Sal's Club. I've been practicing my Beyonce religiously," Max suggested, obviously eager for her to agree.

"Uh, I don't know, Max. Joanne already asked if she could see me later," Alice said, feeling a little bit guilty for abandoning her best friend for sex. She had to acknowledge it wasn't just sex, it was mind-blowing sex, but she knew that Max wouldn't hold any grudges against her for opting to spend the night with a hot woman.

"You little whore!" Max teased. "Don't worry about it. I'll just hang around the club in the hopes of a sugar daddy finding me."

They walked together in light banter and Alice said goodbye to her best friend when they reached his apartment. She still felt bad for ditching Max for sex but knew that she would be happy for him if their roles were reversed.

When Alice reached her apartment, she made herself comfortable on her futon and stared at her phone wondering what to say to Joanne. After a couple of minutes of overthinking, Alice decided to text the first thing that popped into her head.

I'm free tonight. Let me know what time you want me to come over?

And just like that her evening was planned. Alice felt excited about seeing Joanne again. She opened her closet to find something to wear for her visit. She realized that the only clothes she had that would impress someone like Joanne was the work wardrobe that Joanne got her. She couldn't go over to Joanne's place in work clothes. She scanned her closet again and a small smile crossed her face when she came up with plan B.

JOANNE WAS FEELING relaxed and pampered. She didn't realize how much she needed to unwind until the masseuse scolded her for all the stress she was carrying. She thought that after her night with Alice her body would be as relaxed as her mind but apparently not. It wasn't that Joanne was unaware of her unhealthy stressful lifestyle; she just didn't have time for silly things like yoga or meditation.

Joanne got dressed and ready to leave the spa after her various treatments. The wind was picking up and brought on a slight chill to the late afternoon. As she was about to walk over to the waiting Lincoln, she noticed that she received a text from Alice.

I'm free tonight. Let me know what time you want me to come over?

Reading the text brought an instant smile to her face. Joanne rushed to the open car door to take a seat and type back her reply.

I'll pick you up in an hour.

An hour should give Alice enough time to get ready. Joanne called up her favorite restaurant to place an order for dinner. Luckily, she didn't have to wait long as the driver got out to pick up her order. He drove Joanne to Alice's apartment and held the door open for her to exit the vehicle.

As Joanne walked up to the entrance of the building a chubby man wearing a too-tight shirt held the door open for her. She felt disgusted by the way he was looking at her and ignored him as she took the stairs to Alice's apartment.

She knocked on the door, and it was clear from the look on Alice's face that she was expecting the driver instead.

"Um, hi? Please come in," Alice quickly said looking a bit flustered.

"Thank you," Joanne said as she walked into Alice's apartment. Joanne wasn't sure what she was expecting but it wasn't this. The studio apartment was cozy, and it was clear that Alice enjoyed spending time in her home. Something about the tiny apartment reminded Joanne of her childhood home, making it hard to swallow.

"I'll be just a minute," Alice said as she scrambled around her apartment to get her personal items.

"It's a nice place you have here," Joanne said as she looked at the tiny jungle of houseplants on Alice's kitchen counter.

"Thanks, my only problem with this apartment is the drab walls. I'd love to someday paint all the walls in different bright colors. You know, reflect my sparkling personality."

Joanne wasn't the type of person that would paint her walls in crazy wild colors, but the idea suited the little redhead. Joanne always opted for the whitest white paint she could find. She stared at the drab wall in front of her and felt a shiver running down her spine.

"I'm ready when you are," Alice said as she unknowingly rescued Joanne from a dark memory she thought was long gone. For the first time since her arrival, Joanne really looked at the redhead. She was dressed in a navy blue coat with a red scarf tied around her neck.

"After you," Joanne said as she gestured towards the door.

During their drive to Joanne's penthouse, Alice talked about the morning's yoga session she attended and how she was now curious about trying something called goat yoga. Joanne was mesmerized by her enthusiasm even if she didn't understand how anyone would want to exercise with living farm animals.

When they got home, Joanne poured them a drink while her housekeeper set their dinner on the dining table. It was too chilly to have dinner outside, but Joanne loved the fireplace she had in her dining room. If she was being honest, she felt that maybe she had more fireplaces than she actually needed but knowing that her home was warm and toasty made her happy.

The housekeeper informed them that dinner was ready and excused herself for the evening. "Let's sit down for dinner, shall we?" she invited Alice. "Would you like me to take your coat?"

"It's fine, I'll get it," Alice quickly said and started to unbutton the long coat.

Joanne was left breathless as Alice's coat fell open. Underneath, Alice wore nothing but a cherry red pushup bra and matching G-string. Initially, Joanne couldn't wait to feast on the pasta from her favorite Italian restaurant, but suddenly, she was hungry for only one thing.

She removed the coat from Alice's shoulders and loved how Alice looked like a rising phoenix with her red hair and the fire behind her. Joanne couldn't hold back any longer. She pulled Alice closer and they had sex right there in front of the roaring fire.

ALICE KNEW that wearing nothing but lingerie underneath her coat would catch Joanne's attention, but she never imagined that it would ignite a sex-on-the-spot moment. The sex they had in front of the fireplace was raw and rough, and for a moment neither one of them said anything.

After a couple of minutes, Joanne got up from the lush carpet. She held out her hand to help Alice up. "Let's sit down for dinner?" she said.

Instant regret hit Alice. She should have brought something to wear afterwards but she just thought that she would be going home after sex. Alice reached for her coat, but Joanne stopped her from putting it on.

"I like my dinner with a view," Joanne said as she gave Alice a naughty wink.

Alice felt awkward sitting down naked at the elegant dining table, but the way Joanne was looking at her made her feel more comfortable. They made light conversation as they both enjoyed the spectacular meal. Their little pre-dinner romp gave Alice a serious appetite.

Alice helped Joanne clear the table when they were done. "Why don't you make yourself comfortable in my bedroom and I'll bring our dessert?" Joanne asked.

Alice walked through Joanne's penthouse naked. She stopped to look at a painting in the hallway that caught her eye. It was a painting of a lighthouse in the middle of a storm surrounded by darkness. The artist did an excellent job at invoking an emotional response to the piece, and Alice wondered why someone like Joanne would have something hanging on her walls that wasn't necessarily defined as fine art.

She could hear Joanne approach and didn't want to seem nosy so Alice quickly rushed to the oversized bedroom. Alice was still amazed at the fact that her entire apartment could fit into this single bedroom.

"I thought we could have a little picnic for dessert," Joanne said as she placed the tray on her bed.

Alice took a seat next to her. There were chocolate-covered strawberries and whipped cream on the plate. Joanne held out a strawberry for Alice to eat. The way that Joanne was looking at her mouth was making her pussy tingle.

"I need you to lay back on the pillows," Joanne said in a sultry voice.

Eagerly, Alice obeyed and watched as Joanne took the last bite of the chocolate-covered fruit. Joanne scooped up a bit of the cream and traced her cream-covered finger across Alice's lips and down her neck.

Joanne slowly licked the cream from Alice's mouth before following the trail of sweetness down her neck. Alice let out a small moan when Joanne licked the sweet spot close to her ear. Her moan caused Joanne to move her attention to her mouth, and Alice could still taste the sweetness of the dessert on Joanne's tongue.

Alice was craving Joanne's touch and tried to pull her closer, but Joanne had other plans. This time Joanne scooped a bit of the cream onto Alice's breast and just like before she cleaned her soft skin from the stickiness with long, slow licks.

Being extremely aroused, Alice moved her hand down her body to caress her wet pussy. "No touching, Alice," Joanne said. "Keep your hands away from your pussy... Unless you want to be tied up again?"

Although the idea of being bound to Joanne's bed was exciting, she would much rather be touching Joanne's soft skin. With her eyes closed and lost in the sensations of Joanne's expert lips, Alice gave a slight jolt at the instant coldness covering her pussy. She looked down and saw that Joanne must have dumped the entire bowl of whipped cream on her.

"Now hold still before everything melts," Joanne said as she moved her head to Alice's cream-covered pussy. She was licking and sucking every inch of her, giving extra attention to her tingling labia. Alice didn't know how much more she could take. "Please," she said with ragged breath.

"Please what, Alice?" Joanne asked, waiting for her to say it out loud.

"Please fuck me already," Alice said and with that Joanne pushed her fingers hard inside of her. Enough to make her gasp. But, she liked it.

"Keep your eyes on me, Alice," Joanne said as she began to grind her own pussy against Alice's thigh while her fingers began to fuck deep inside of her. Joanne's grinding turned harder by the minute and when Joanne ordered her to come, Alice's body wasted mere seconds before eagerly responding and climaxing loudly.

Alice felt Joanne orgasm and gush on her leg simultaneously. Wow, they had some serious sexual connection going on.

Joanne smiled down at her and said, "I'll get the shower running."

JOANNE LED Alice to the large, steam-filled shower. Normally, she would think an act like taking a shower together would be too intimate, but they were both covered in the sticky sugar from the whipped cream and she wouldn't send Alice home like that today. She watched the sexy Alice as she leaned forward to feel the spray of the shower head on her back.

The sight made Joanne's knees feel weak. She pushed Alice against the wall and with her tits pressed against the cold shower tiles, Joanne used her free hand to fuck her pussy hard and rough.

Joanne didn't plan on fucking her again, but she

needed to feel Alice's pussy muscles tighten around her fingers just one more time. "Remember, Alice, if you need me to stop, just say red," she reminded the woman she held pushed up against the wall.

Getting no reply from Alice except loud moans encouraged Joanne to increase her onslaught. She inserted more fingers, curled down at her G spot, feeling Alice stretched out for her, feeling her knuckles hitting Alice's pubic bone. Alice moaned harder, causing Joanne to increase her pace and force of thrust, and just as she was beginning to think it might be too much, Alice let out a scream, and gushed hot and wet down her inner thighs almost collapsing as Joanne used her left hand and her body to catch her. Joanne held the fingers of her right hand still in place inside Alice giving Alice a few seconds to catch her breath.

"If you want me to stop, say now.." Joanne began to move her fingers again pressing Alice's G spot and looking at her perfect little ass.

Alice began to moan again so Joanne's fingers began to fuck her again. It was barely any time at all before Alice was screaming and gushing and weak at the knees again and Joanne smiled in utter satisfaction.

Fuck, she only gets more and more beautiful.

When it was clear that Alice was done, Joanne turned her around, holding her up, the steam and spray from the shower surrounding them still. She looked at Alice's half-glazed-over eyes. "Are you okay?" she asked, looking for any signs of distress.

Alice gave her the biggest smile that she's ever seen and replied, "I'm so much more than okay."

10

Back at the office, Alice and Joanne tried to sneak in as many sexual moments as they could. The excitement of being caught kept Alice on edge but deep down she knew that Joanne would never let anything jeopardize her career.

They saw each other every night since the first night that Joanne invited her over. Usually, by now, Alice's libido would have calmed down a bit, but everything was new and different with Joanne. Joanne even came over to her place a couple of times and Alice was even getting used to being driven home after they had sex.

She was sure that the driver knew what was happening but he never said a word about it. He was always professional, and Alice appreciated the fact that she didn't have to feel judged by him. It was strange that they never conversed but it also created a barrier between them that she valued.

Alice stopped by the coffee shop to get Joanne her morning coffee. By now the staff knew her by name and they usually had her morning order ready when she came in. The large tip she usually added to Joanne's credit card ensured that she always received VIP treatment but that's not why she did it. She knew from experience how ungrateful customers could be and didn't envy the coffee shop employees.

Alice walked towards Joanne's office wearing a goofy grin. She was in a good mood and couldn't wait to see Joanne. She found it strange that the receptionist wasn't at his desk as usual but ignored it and walked to the closed door. Just as she was about to open the door, she heard voices from within. She didn't mean to eavesdrop but couldn't help but listen to the conversation on the other side.

"I can't wait to spend the weekend with you. It's been way too long," she heard a strange woman say.

"I'll be there on the Thursday. I still have a few things to finalize before I can join you, but I will let you know once I leave," Joanne said.

Joanne's appointments and scheduling was her responsibility. Alice knew that not only did this woman not have an appointment this morning, there was nothing scheduled for any Thursdays with any woman.

Alice could hear that the women was approaching the door and didn't want to be caught standing there listening to their conversation. She quickly knocked on the door pretending as if she just arrived.

She opened the door and saw a gorgeous, tall brunette with long, luscious hair standing next to Joanne. The brunette looked like she could be on any magazine cover and made Alice feel dull and boring.

"Good morning. I'm sorry, I didn't realize that you had

a guest; I didn't mean to interrupt," Alice quickly said as she was about to turn around.

"No worries," the beautiful brunette replied, "I was just leaving." She gave Alice a flashing smile as she and Joanne walked out of the office towards the elevators. The beautiful brunette wore a tailored pantsuit with killer heels.

Alice was curious about this woman but didn't want to ask Joanne about her. She didn't want to give the impression that she was jealous, although if she was being honest with herself, she might be. Even if it was just a little bit. She knew that what she had with Joanne was supposed to be no strings attached but she didn't like the idea of Joanne being involved with another woman, especially someone that was the complete opposite of Alice.

"Thanks for the coffee," Joanne said as she closed the door behind her upon her return. She took a seat at her desk and stared at Alice. "Is everything alright?" she asked Alice with concern in her voice.

"Yes, yes I'm fine," Alice lied. "Why do you ask?"

From the look Joanne gave her, Alice could tell that Joanne wasn't buying it. "Because you don't seem quite yourself this morning," Joanne said.

"It's nothing. I just woke up with a headache. I'll feel better once the ibuprofen kicks in," Alice said as she picked up the files from the desk that Joanne was finished with.

Joanne got up and took Alice into her arms. She gave her a kiss on the top of her head and said, "Do you want to know what helps for headaches?"

"Let me guess. You're going to tell me that sex is the miracle drug," Alice said with a smile.

"No, not sex. If sex was the cure for headaches, humans would be fucking all day every day," Joanne said.

"Fine, I give up. What helps with headaches?" Alice asked.

"Orgasms," Joanne teased.

"Isn't that the same thing, Miss Morgan?" Alice asked.

"Not at all. It's possible to reach an orgasm without sex just as easily as it is to have sex without reaching an orgasm," Joanne said, wiggling her eyebrows.

"You have a valid point, I suppose," Alice replied.

Alice felt bad for lying to Joanne, but it was better than telling her that she was jealous of the beautiful brunette. She wasn't the type to fake a headache but desperate times called for desperate measures.

"As you know, my day is pretty busy, unfortunately, but if you want I can come over to your place and provide relief for your headache after work?" Joanne said as she traced her finger along Alice's neckline.

It felt good knowing that Joanne still wanted to see her tonight even after the visit from the brunette. Alice wanted to say yes but then remembered that she wouldn't be available. "Actually, I already have something happening tonight. I committed to this long before I started working here."

Disappointment showed on Joanne's face. "Oh, okay," she said and started to turn around to take her seat at her desk.

It wasn't that Alice was looking for an excuse but she wasn't sure if Joanne would want to join her in after-hours activities that didn't necessarily include sex. Deciding to bite the bullet, Alice said, "Why don't you join me tonight? I have a friend who is in a band and they are performing at a bar. I promised that I would go out and support him. I know it might not be your scene but I'd like for you to join me. If you wanted to."

Alice felt nervous as she waited for Joanne to answer her. She promised Max that she would be at the bar tonight, but she also wanted to spend time with Joanne. Would Joanne really say no to her invitation? Alice was scared that she might be making a fool of herself by asking Joanne out.

"Yeah, going out to loud, overcrowded bars is not really my scene, thanks," Joanne said as she turned her attention to her computer.

"Oh, okay," Alice said, disappointed. "The offer is standing if you decide to change your mind. I'm going down to finance to submit your files. I'll be back in a few minutes," Alice said and walked away before Joanne could see the disappointment in her eyes.

JOANNE WAS LOOKING FORWARD to spending yet another night with Alice. She was getting used to having her fantasies fulfilled every night. Alice's invitation caught her completely off guard. She couldn't remember the last time she went out to a bar or club, never mind going out on a date.

Would it really be considered a date though? Alice didn't say it was a date, she just asked her to come along to support one of her friends. But that in itself was another issue that Joanne wanted to avoid. Meeting friends created expectations, and she was clear that what was happening between them was just for fun.

Joanne stared down at her calendar. It was almost thanksgiving and she still had plans with her own friends for the thanksgiving weekend. That was why Lindsay dropped by this morning, to ensure all their plans are finalized. If she couldn't imagine spending one night without having sex with Alice, how would she survive a whole weekend?

Walking over to the window overlooking the busy city, Joanne was caught between a rock and a hard place. She wanted to spend the night with Alice but she couldn't expect her to let her friends down because Joanne was insatiable.

Would it really be that bad to spend time in a public setting with Alice? Maybe it would be okay if she made it clear that it was not a date? They could go to the stupid bar and afterwards she could have her way with Alice.

Right at that moment, Alice walked into her office again. "Mr. Franklin wanted me to remind you about the Titan file that is still outstanding. He needs it signed off before the close of business today," Alice announced.

"Alice?" Joanne said as she stared out at the view from her window.

"Yes?" Alice replied, her voice filled with curiosity.

"Did you really mean it when you said you wanted me to join you tonight or were you just feeling sorry for me? I don't want to intrude on your evening and I definitely don't want to be there out of pity," Joanne said.

"I wouldn't have asked you to join me if I didn't mean it. Sex with you is great. Don't get me wrong, but sex is not always necessary to have a good time, you know," Alice stated the obvious.

"I know. I just wanted to make sure." Joanne was stalling. "And it's not a date, right?" Joanne asked.

Alice rolled her eyes at Joanne's question. "No Joanne, it's not a date."

"I see," Joanne said, still unsure if she should agree or not.

"We don't even have to stay long if you don't want to. After the first couple of songs, I'll tell Max that I'm leaving and then we can go back to your place if you want," Alice tried to convince her.

"Let's see how the day goes. I don't want to commit to anything if something else might mess up your plans," Joanne said, still unsure if she should go.

Joanne wasn't making excuses when she said that she had a busy day ahead. When Alice brought in her lunch, she could hardly believe how much time passed since their discussion that morning. Before she met Alice, this would be the kind of day that Joanne lived for. She thrived on being busy but today was both a blessing and a curse.

She was still unsure if she should join Alice at the bar. She told Alice she could leave early and that she would confirm later this afternoon. Time was running out and she had to make a decision. Tired of weighing the pros and cons and overthinking things, Joanne decided to try it out and she quickly sent a text to inform Alice.

What time would you like me to meet you tonight?

Joanne hit send before she could change her mind. She saw that Alice was already sending a reply to her text. It read:

I'm so happy that you're coming. I'll send you the address and meet you outside (since it's not a date don't expect me to pick you up) xo A

Joanne smiled at the witty message from Alice. Panic started to set in the moment reality hit her. She was going to a bar. Joanne had no idea what to wear and quickly arranged with the driver to take her to her favorite clothing store.

Over the years, the manager at the store knew her well enough to always find the perfect outfits for her. When she told him that she needed an outfit to go out to a bar and see a band, the manager was strangely dumbstruck and excited by being able to recommended something different from the elegant business outfits or gala dresses he would usually suggest.

Joanne looked at all the different outfits that he put together for her. She would never be caught dead in any of them. Sure she enjoyed looking at other woman in these kinds of sexy, edgy outfits but wearing any just wasn't her thing. For a moment, Joanne wondered if it was too late to cancel her evening out with Alice.

Just then the manager showed her something different and Joanne knew that she would feel comfortable wearing it. Without trying it on, she had the items added to her bill and left the store to wait in the car for the driver to return with her shopping bags.

While waiting, Joanne took out her phone to check her messages. Sure enough, she received a message from Alice. It was the address of the bar she was supposed to meet her at. Joanne opened the location link, and the moment that her map loaded on her screen, her heart stopped. She could feel the blood drain from her face and was finding it hard to breathe.

Joanne swore to herself that she would never return to that part of town. It was too late to back out now. Maybe enough time has passed for her to be more comfortable in that neighborhood? Maybe it changed enough to not bring back all the bad memories. Maybe it will be too dark for her to remember the reason for her avoiding those streets?

As the driver got in, Joanne closed her eyes and took a

deep breath. She tried to relax and focus on Alice. She would keep her mind on Alice and everything would be fine. Joanne repeated this mantra over and over until she could feel her heart settle in her chest. She tried to tell herself to relax and just enjoy the evening for what it was. Going back didn't mean she was going back in history.

11

"I can't believe that you're on a date with your boss tonight," Max said as the rest of his band was setting up their equipment for the sound check before the doors opened.

"Technically, it's not a date, Max," Alice quickly said.

"Yeah right," Max replied.

"I just thought it might be fun to show Joanne that there is more to life than just work, you know," Alice said.

"Of course, you invited her to save humanity," Max said as he rolled his eyes.

"Well, it's better than having to be here all by myself while you're on stage," Alice said, looking at the time on her phone. She wouldn't admit it to Max or even herself, but she was excited to see Joanne tonight.

Alice was surprised when Joanne agreed. She knew that this wasn't Joanne's scene, but maybe a change of pace would do her good. Over the past couple of weeks, Alice was growing more curious about Joanne every day. Although their time together was truly mind-blowing,

Alice wondered what made this woman tick. She sometimes saw glimpses of a softer, kinder woman but that would quickly be replaced by the bitchy, bossy, cold-hearted woman that everyone knew.

"Okay. Sound check is done. I'm so nervous!" Max said, all giddy, interrupting her thoughts.

"That's my cue. Don't be nervous, Maxie, you're going to be great." Alice gave Max a hug to wish him luck for his performance and walked to the exit to wait for Joanne.

Outside the bar, people were already waiting in line to enter for tonight's show. This was definitely the biggest crowd that Max had ever played for. She smiled at the bouncer who was guarding the entrance like a secret service agent. That is, if secret service agents were birthed by giants.

Alice quickly checked her phone again. Although the show wasn't due to start for another hour or so, Joanne was already 10 minutes late to their agreed time. She had no messages from Joanne and hoped that she didn't decide to just flake on her.

Right at that moment, Alice saw the familiar black Lincoln pull up. Alice couldn't keep herself from smiling. The driver walked around to open the back door for Joanne and when she stepped out Alice was left breathless.

Alice always thought of Joanne as a sexy woman, but this version of Joanne in front of her oozed sex. She was wearing tight black leather pants with boots and a jacket with a corset underneath that not only emphasized her tiny waist and voluptuous ass but thrust her breasts out like two perfectly round orbs. Joanne's beautiful long icy blonde locks were braided into a Viking-style braid and the smoky eye and long lashes made her blue eyes stand out.

When Joanne noticed her staring, she gave Alice a small smile and turned around for her to take everything in. "Wow, you look amazing," Alice said as she reached her. She couldn't take her eyes off of Joanne's transformation.

"Thank you," Joanne said confidently as always. "You look beautiful tonight."

Alice glanced down at the dress she was wearing. She didn't think that the tight, silver sequined dress was anything special but she knew that it made her look and feel good. "Thank you, would you like to go inside?"

"It's better than standing out here all night," Joanne said.

She took Joanne's hand and led her into the bar, walking past the long line of strangers and the giant secret service bouncer. They took a seat at the bar as they waited for the band to start. It was loud but if Joanne felt out of place, she didn't show it.

After a few drinks, the band took to the stage. They didn't notice the swarm of people entering the bar as they waited. Again, Alice grabbed Joanne's hand and dragged her to the front of the stage. She was excited to experience this with Joanne. The music was loud and Alice knew every song word for word. She could see Max was having a blast and he gave her a thumbs up when they made eye contact in the crowd.

Joanne was moving to the music, but it was clear that she wasn't going to let go the way that Alice was. Joanne oozed sex appeal as she danced to the music, and Alice noticed a number of men and woman staring at her in the crowd. When the band announced their break, Max came down towards them and Alice introduced him to Joanne.

They made small talk for a few minutes. Alice couldn't tell what Max thought of Joanne since he was being his super polite self rather than his real self. What Alice knew was that Max and Joanne would probably never end up being friends.

It seemed obvious that Joanne might be a bit overwhelmed by the evening although she didn't say anything, and once Max had to get back to the stage, Alice asked, "Would you like to get out of here?"

"Isn't your friend still playing?" Joanne asked.

"Yeah, but I've been to all his other shows. He won't mind if I slip away," Alice said.

"If you're sure," Joanne said.

"Come on, let's get out of here," Alice said as she led Joanne towards the exit.

The night was chilly and the darkness and muffled sounds from the crowded bar filled the air. Just as the driver pulled the Lincoln closer Alice said, "Why don't we get some fresh air before leaving?"

Joanne looked at her surroundings. She seemed uncomfortable. "It looks more dangerous than it is, I promise," Alice said, trying to put her at ease. It was true. Although it wasn't the best part of town, it was relatively safe, especially here at the pier where cops patrolled throughout the night.

"We'll be back in a few minutes," Joanne told the driver.

They walked towards the end of the pier and took a seat on one of the benches. The noise from the bar was in the distance and the moonlight that was reflecting on the water looked like a silver sliver on black ink. There weren't a lot of people around them. The odd couple making out on the pier and a group of teenagers smoking cigarettes without being caught.

They sat in silence for a while. Alice was beginning to feel uncomfortable by Joanne being so quiet. "Would you rather go back?" Alice asked.

"It's fine," Joanne said as she let out a sigh. It was obvious that something was wrong.

"If you're cold or uncomfortable I really don't mind going back," Alice said. She was surprised by Joanne's sudden solemn mood.

"It's not that. It's just..." Joanne took a noticeable big breath. "I want to show you something." She said as she got up from the bench.

Alice walked beside her back towards the waiting car. Joanne gave an address to the driver and sat in silence next to Alice in the back seat. The car was filled with tension, but Alice didn't want to be the one to break the silence. She had no idea where they were going but trusted Joanne, so she stared out of her window and waited.

After about a fifteen-minute drive, the Lincoln stopped in front of an abandoned apartment building. Joanne got out of the car and held open the door for Alice. Alice felt uncomfortable knowing that the building was probably housing a couple of homeless people or drug addicts. She never ventured away from the pier when she came to this part of town.

Breaking the silence, Alice nervously asked, "What is this place?"

Joanne looked up to the top story of the building. She took another deep breath before speaking. "This is where I grew up," Joanne said.

Alice was shocked. For some reason she imagined someone like Joanne growing up in the life of luxury. The last place she would have ever imagined Joanne to grow up would be in this part of town, not to mention housing like this. She could tell that even years ago this building was home to the lower income population of the city.

She looked at Joanne and saw a single tear run down her face. Alice wasn't sure what to do. "Are you okay?" she asked in a hushed voice.

"Yeah, let's get in the car before we both catch a cold," Joanne quickly said as she wiped the tear away.

Once inside, Joanne rolled up the screen between them and the driver. They sat in silence for a while. Alice was waiting for Joanne to speak. She wasn't sure if this was something that Joanne wanted to talk about so she waited for her to break the silence.

"I lived in that building until I turned eighteen," Joanne said as she stared out of the window. "My parents, two brothers and twin sister all lived in a one-bedroom apartment on the top floor. We all slept in the living/dining room on the floor with only a curtain providing some privacy to each one."

Alice didn't know what to say. She grew up in a happy home with a white picket fence. She didn't grow up rich but was always safe and well cared for. She was healthy, well fed and was never left wanting for anything. She took Joanne's hand in hers, trying give her some comfort.

Joanne continued, "To this day I remember going to bed hungry. I remember having to spend endless nights in darkness because my parents couldn't afford to pay for electricity. A lot of the nights, my sister and I would walk down to the pier and just stare at the lighthouse in the distance wishing that we could leave all of this behind us. We would make up stories about how we would have a fairy tale ending and live happily ever after."

Still staring out of the window, Alice could see Joanne's tears flowing freely. Joanne took another deep breath and continued, "My sister killed herself when we were 17, she had said to me that she was tired of fighting the constant storms in her life. I knew how hard our lives were but I never imagined that my sister would take her own life."

Alice did not expect any of this. "I'm so sorry about your sister. It must have been so hard to lose someone close to you in such a way."

"It was," Joanne said, "but because of her I am where I am today. Losing her pushed me to work even harder to get out of that place. I studied every free moment I had and got a full scholarship for college. I left the day after I graduated and never looked back. Tonight was the first time I ever returned."

"But what about your family?" Alice asked.

"Both my parents turned to drugs after my sister's death. My mother couldn't cope with her passing and my dad couldn't cope with my mother's grief. I heard a few years ago that my dad died. I don't know where my mum is now. I couldn't cope with the drugs, you see. My eldest brother is currently locked up serving a 25-year sentence on various charges and my other brother chose to live on the streets amongst the homeless the last I heard," Joanne said.

"I'm sorry to hear that, Joanne," Alice said.

"Don't be sorry for me. I'm not. I admit that I had a tough childhood and probably endured more than most, but I fought to reach the top. That's why it's so important to me to keep going. I won't ever allow myself to return to this life," Joanne said as she looked at Alice.

It all made sense to Alice now. The reason why Joanne was always so driven and never allowed herself any free time was because she was fighting to keep her past in the past. Joanne probably thought that if she slacked just the tiniest bit that she would lose everything and end up back here.

"May I ask you something?" Alice asked.

"Sure," Joanne replied.

"The painting of the lighthouse in your hallway—" Alice started her question.

Not letting Alice finish her question, Joanne said, "It reminds me of my sister. Of the lighthouse we use to look at from the pier. Of the storms we both had to face growing up. The storms that became too much for her. It reminds me to stay strong. It reminds me to keep fighting," Joanne explained.

Everything was starting to make sense now and Alice could feel her heart swell. She reached her hand across in the dark and squeezed Joanne's hand. She admired this woman even more and she respected the fact that she truly worked for what she had in life. Joanne wasn't just given a wealthy lifestyle and respectful job. She earned it. She fought for it.

She never gave up despite her hardships, and even though no one else knew it, Alice knew that the bitchy ice queen that Joanne portrayed was nothing more than a protective wall to keep herself strong.

In that moment, Alice wished she could show Joanne that she didn't have to always stay strong. That she could let her walls down and let others help her through her storms.

As the driver parked the car, Joanne looked down at the sleeping Alice on her shoulder. She drifted off a couple of minutes ago and Joanne felt bad for waking her but they couldn't stay inside the car all night.

"Wakey wakey, sleepy head," Joanne teased.

Confused and half asleep, Alice opened her eyes. "I'm sorry. I didn't mean to fall asleep," she quickly said as she sat up straight.

"No problem," Joanne replied.

Alice looked out the window and when she saw them parked outside her apartment building, she looked sad. "I thought we were going back to your place," she said to Joanne.

Joanne got out of the car and held the door open for Alice. "I thought that maybe we could spend our time together here tonight? You know, a change of scenery."

Quickly, Alice embraced her with a huge smile. "Yes! That sounds great. Come in, please. I'm so sorry if it's messy."

Alice excitedly led them to her apartment. She let Joanne walk in and locked the door behind them. "Could I get you something to drink?" she asked.

"No, thank you, Alice, I'm fine," Joanne said as she stalked towards Alice with a predatory smile. She took Alice into her arms and for a moment she stared into her eyes, staring into her beautiful soul. Joanne kissed her tenderly.

The air around them was filled with electricity, and Joanne walked Alice backwards until the back of her legs made contact with her bed. Joanne lifted the bottom of the silver sequin dress over Alice's head and lightly pushed Alice onto the bed.

Joanne stripped off herself and got on top of Alice on the bed.

This time when she kissed her, she kissed her deeply, and passionately.

Something felt different. Joanne couldn't explain it, but she wanted touch and caress every inch of Alices sexy body. She wanted more. It wasn't just hunger, whatever was happening between them was making every nerve in her body ache, in a good way.

Alice flipped her on her back and placed her leg in between Joanne's thighs. Joanne could feel Alice grind against her and when Alice's hand stroked her aching pussy it didn't take long for Joanne to come. Still out of breath, Joanne watched as Alice took her hand off Joanne's body, ran it down her own body, and while straddling Joanne, made herself climax as she stared into Joanne's eyes. Joanne didn't even mention the fact that Alice had orgasmed without being told to or given permission to.

In the afterglow of their climax, Alice asked, "Would you like me to order us some pizza?"

"I could eat," Joanne said.

As they ate pizza on Alice's bed, they talked about everyday things, like a normal couple would do. Alice told her about how she met Max and they laughed together when she told Joanne about the time Max got drunk in a lesbian bar and won first place in a Celine Dion karaoke competition.

When Joanne noticed the sunrise approaching, she called the driver to pick her up. Alice seemed disappointed in her leaving but she knew the rules. When the driver arrived, she kissed Alice goodbye and walked down the stairs. Joanne could tell that something had changed between them. She just didn't know what it was, or perhaps she did know, but she just really didn't want to admit it to herself.

12

Joanne was driving along I-95 in her midnight blue Aston Martin. She saw the exit towards Cape Cod and knew that she reached her halfway mark. Initially, Joanne was planning on taking her private jet to visit her friends for thanksgiving weekend, but the long drive gave her some much-needed alone time to think about her current situation.

Since the night she went to the bar with Alice, they spent every single minute together that they possibly could. Usually after work they would have dinner, go back to her penthouse to spend some time together, which always ended up in amazing sex, before saying goodnight and having the driver drop Alice off at her apartment.

Alice even managed to convince her to go to the movies with her. It was a silly horror film with all the usual jump scares, and although Joanne didn't particularly enjoy the movie for what it was, she enjoyed the experience with Alice. It was nice living a bit of a normal life for a change.

She was enjoying spending time with Alice no matter

what they did. She thought back to the night she attempted to get revenge on Alice for having to sit through the stupid horror film by taking her out to the opera. She thought Alice would be bored to death, but it turned out that she loved every minute. Alice said that it was her first time going to the opera and never knew what all the fuss was about until that night.

Joanne smiled as she thought back to how Alice talked nonstop all the way back to her penthouse and how the driver winced at her pitchy attempt of a La Boheme song. Alice never failed to amuse her.

Joanne knew that Alice had no definite plans for this weekend, other than spending it with Max, and she could have easily invited both of them to join her and her friends in Martha's Vineyard, but Joanne needed a break from whatever was happening between Alice and herself. She needed to clear her head. Alice was getting under her skin and she could not allow it.

From past experience, Joanne knew that romantic relationships were a waste of time and always ended in heartbreak. She was already spending less time in the office while gallivanting around with Alice and couldn't allow Alice to be such a distraction.

It was nice spending so much time with Alice, but they had to reinforce boundaries. The next couple of days apart would be good for both of them to get a better perspective on their business and personal boundaries.

Joanne's cellphone rang over the Aston Martin's speakers. "Hello," she answered by pressing a button on her steering wheel. It was her friend, Lindsay. "I just reached Cape Cod. I should be there in, let's say, a little over two hours? Okay. Good, see you then."

Joanne disconnected the call and turned her attention

to the long road she still had ahead of her. She refused to let the redhead consume her thoughts this weekend and instead she tried to picture her friends and their beautiful house waiting for her. She thought of all the delicious dishes that she knew Lindsay would be preparing and the late night conversations they would have on the deck over a few glasses of wine.

To get Alice out of her head, Joanne switched on her radio and selected a playlist of easy listening music that she knew wouldn't distract her from her drive. She looked forward to relaxing this weekend. She looked forward to clearing her mind and returning focus and control to her life.

ALICE WALKED into her apartment carrying the takeout she and Max got after their volunteer shift at the homeless shelter. This was a yearly ritual they begin after Max's boyfriend Mark passed away in a car accident four years ago. Helping the less fortunate was not only the right thing to do, but it distracted Max from his hurtful past.

Most people thought of Max as a slutty drama queen scared of commitment, but Alice knew him better. Max didn't want to let anyone close. He surrounded himself with as many new interests as he possibly could to try and forget about Mark. Alice didn't blame him. Their love was truly the kind of love that everybody dreams of. Mark died in Max's arms before paramedics could arrive and they never found the driver that killed Mark.

"So, where is Frosty this weekend?" Max said as he locked the door behind him.

"Max, that's not nice. You know her name is Joanne,"

Alice said as she started to unpack their meal on her too-small table.

"Yeah, I know, but Frosty suits her better. She's crazy scary," Max said.

"She's not that bad. You've met her," Alice replied.

"I talked to her for ten minutes. That's it. Not much you can tell about someone you talk to for ten minutes in a crowed bar, is there?" Max asked.

"I suppose not," Alice sighed. She didn't have the energy for this right now. She's been up all night thinking about this weekend and how strange it was going to be to not see Joanne until Monday at the office.

"I guess if I looked as good in a pair of Jimmy Choo boots as she did, I would probably be a bitch too," Max said as he strutted towards the kitchen to grab glasses from her cupboard.

"Max, you're a bitch in any case. No Jimmy Choos required," Alice replied.

"Yeah, but designer clothes would make me look better while being a bitch," Max said with a wink.

Alice and Max took their seats at her tiny dining table. Alice wondered what Joanne was doing at the moment. She was hoping that Joanne arrived safe after her long drive, and for a moment she thought of sending her a text but didn't want to overstep.

"You never told me; where's Joanne this weekend?" Max said before taking a huge bite of his dinner.

Alice shrugged trying not to look too interested in his question. "She said something about visiting friends in Martha's Vineyard."

"Oh my god, Alice! She has friends in Martha's Vineyard and you couldn't get us an invite." Max said too loud.

"Max, I can't just ask my boss to drag us along, can I?

Besides, you and I already have our Thanksgiving rituals," Alice said.

"So now Joanne is just your boss, huh?" Max asked.

Alice didn't want to have this conversation with Max. "She's always been my boss. So what if we fuck sometimes after hours?"

A slow smile crossed Max's face. "I knew it."

"What? What did you know?" Alice asked, slightly irritated with Max's questioning.

"You like her," Max said, raising his eyebrows. "You really like her."

"I do not. Now shut up and fill our glasses," Alice quickly said. She should have known that Max would eventually pick up on her feelings for Joanne.

"Why don't you talk to her about how you're feeling?" Max said as he filled her glass.

"Because it's nothing, Max. It's just a momentary infatuation that will probably pass by Monday. Besides, she made it clear from the beginning that this was a no-strings-attached arrangement, remember? You still told me to go for it," Alice said, annoyed.

Max took Alice's hand in his. "Alice, if it's real and if it's what your heart wants, go for it. Life is too short to ignore love. Life is too short to not experience love."

Alice lost her appetite and was merely pushing around the food on her plate. She wanted to tell Joanne how she felt about her, but she didn't want to lose what they had. Maybe she's right in thinking it's just a silly crush and that it would probably be gone by the time she sees Joanne on Monday. They were spending a lot of time together and this time apart would give her a break to clear her thoughts.

After dinner, Alice and Max got comfortable on her

futon. There was a movie marathon that Max wanted to watch and Alice knew that would mean no further interrogations from him. She made herself comfortable, but barely five minutes into the first movie, her mind drifted to thoughts of Joanne.

"Dinner was amazing. Thank you, Lindsey," Joanne said as she took her seat outside on the deck. It was a beautiful night and Joanne could feel herself relax in the fresh air.

"Are you sure you don't want some more dessert?" her friend asked.

"I promise if I had any room left to fit it in, I would say yes," Joanne replied.

"Aunty Jo, can you read us a bedtime story?" Lindsey's six-year-old asked as her four-year-old sister was holding on to her princess book for dear life. They were the splitting imagine of their mother with long dark braids and pink princess pajamas.

"Why don't you ask Daddy to read to you? Aunty Jo had a very long day driving all the way here to come visit us," Lindsey quickly said.

Joanne leaned forward and took the little girl's hands in her own. "I promise that I will read you *two* stories tomorrow night. Mommy and I need to catch up on a few things tonight. Is that alright?" Joanne asked the girl in front of her.

"Okay, Aunty Jo," the girl said.

"Come on, let me tuck you in and then daddy can read you and your sister a story. Say goodnight to Aunty Jo," Lindsay instructed.

"Night, Aunty Jo," the two girls said in unison as they walked inside with their mother.

Joanne smiled to herself as she watched them leave with Lindsay. Her friend was probably the best mom she knew. They knew each other since college. Back then, this was not how either of them would picture their lives to be.

Lindsay used to be a Michelin star chef in London and the day she found out she was pregnant, she resigned and moved back home to be a full-time mother. Joanne didn't know how anyone could give up a promising future like that to raise a couple of babies. It wasn't as if Lindsay and her husband couldn't afford a full-time nanny or au pair.

"Sorry about that," Lindsay said as she took her seat next to Joanne again.

"No problem. They are two beautiful girls, Linds. You are doing a great job," Joanne said.

"Thanks. It's not always easy, but it's definitely worth it. You know, I always thought that you would be a great mother," Lindsay said.

"Me? No thanks. I'm way too old for that. Besides my business is my baby, you know that," Joanne replied.

"Yes, so you keep saying. Something about you seems different though," Lindsay said as she looked at Joanne over her wine glass.

Joanne looked at her with a frown. "What do you mean?"

Lindsay shrugged and said, "I don't know. You seem, how should I put this...um, lighter?"

"If that is your way of telling me I've lost weight, you're doing an awful job," Joanne teased.

"That's not what I meant and you know it," Lindsay laughed.

Joanne suspected that her friend was able to pick up

on the change in her demeanor. She just didn't think it would happen so soon after her arrival. She was trying her best to think of a way to change the topic before Lindsay wanted to get too deep into things.

"What's her name?" Lindsay suddenly said.

"What makes you think there is someone?" Joanne said as she almost choked on a sip of her wine.

"Oh please, Joanne, I've known you for years. I can tell when you're in love," Lindsay said with a smile.

"I'm *not* in love, okay. I've just been spending some time with a woman who agreed to a no-strings, mutually beneficial arrangement," Joanne quickly said.

Lindsay was smiling. "So does your fuck buddy have a name?"

"Of course she has a name," Joanne said, trying to not give her friend any more details. This weekend was supposed to make her forget about the redhead back home. Telling her friend about Alice was not going to help her forget.

"Well? What's her name, Joanne? Come on, tell me. Please? I'm an old, bored, married housewife desperate for some juicy stories," Lindsay said with pleading eyes.

Joanne rolled her eyes at her friend's dramatic plea. "Fine. Her name is Alice."

"Oh my god! The redhead from your office!" Lindsay interrupted her.

Joanne forgot that Lindsay bumped into Alice during her last visit. She closed her eyes and continued. "Yes, the redhead from my office. It was something that evolved. I have fun, she has fun and that's it. You know that I do not have time to waste on stupid things like romance and relationships."

"Joanne, I don't want you to end up alone someday. I

wish you could see that it is possible to have love in your life and still be the fabulous CEO that you are," Lindsay said.

"You mean like you? You quit your job when you found out you were pregnant," Joanne said.

"That's not fair. That was my choice. No one forced me to quit and move back home. I wanted to be a full-time mom, Joanne. If I wanted to return to work tomorrow, I could do that easily. I could start my own thing here in Martha's Vineyard or write a cookbook if I wanted to, but I don't. I'm at my happiest when I am with my girls. All I'm saying is, there is more to life than work and I want you to have it all," Lindsay said as Joanne stared at the horizon.

"I think I should go to bed. I'm tired after the long drive," Joanne excused herself. "Goodnight, Linds."

"Goodnight, Jo," Lindsay replied softly.

Lying in bed, Joanne thought about what Lindsay said about having it all. Could she really be with Alice and still be a successful CEO? As Joanne closed her eyes, the image of the dark, overcrowded, one-bedroom apartment filled her mind. No. She couldn't allow anything to distract her. There was no way she could risk her life to return to where she came from.

13

Alice was excited to return to the office. She couldn't wait to see Joanne. She was already downstairs waiting for the driver to pick her up. Alice thought back to the last couple of days, and she could no longer deny that she was growing attached to Joanne. She thought that a few days apart would make her realize that it was all in her head when, in fact, the separation from Joanne had the opposite effect.

She also knew that she would have to play it cool. She couldn't show Joanne that she was developing feelings for her until she could figure out a way to determine if Joanne feels the same. A small part of her felt that Joanne also had feelings for her, but she didn't want to pursue anything until she knew for sure.

When the driver parked the Town Car, Alice quickly walked to the café to get Joanne her latte. Even the shop owner mentioned her exceptional good mood this morning. She just said that she must have needed the Thanksgiving break more than she thought she did. As usual, she added an enormous tip for the staff on Joanne's credit card and walked towards the office building.

Alice got out of the elevator and walked straight to Joanne's office. She knocked on the door softly before slowly opening the door. And there she was. Dressed in her usual sexy business attire. Alice loved it when Joanne wore suits to work, especially on days like today when she had her long hair pulled back and walked around in smoking hot stilettoes.

When Joanne noticed her, she gave her a big smile. "Good morning, Alice," she said.

"Good morning, Miss Morgan," Alice replied and placed Joanne's latte on her desk. "Did you have a good weekend?"

"I did, thank you. How was yours?" Joanne asked as she took a sip of her coffee.

Alice gave a small shrug. "I suppose it was okay. Max and I were basically just lazing around all weekend."

"I like your outfit today," Joanne said.

Alice chose the dress on purpose. She knew it was one of Joanne's favorites. "Thank you, would you like to get started with today's schedule?" Alice asked.

"Yes, please take your seat," Joanne said with a smile.

Alice knew that this was Joanne's favorite time of their workday. When she sat in her high stool giving Joanne a full view of her entire body. In time, Alice grew to love the way Joanne would look at her while in her stool. It was how every workday started. It was how the intensity of their lust grew. It was how they conveyed their desires without saying a word.

By lunch time, Alice was so worked up that she thought she would lose her mind. After their morning meeting, Joanne was constantly in either some meeting or trying to do damage control on a project that wasn't running the way it should be. Alice had thought the weekend without Joanne's touch was torture but being with her physically and not being able to satisfy her needs was what true torture was really about.

Alice couldn't remember a single day that she was running around as much as she was today and her feet were killing her. She tried to tell herself that her workday was almost over. That it was almost time to join Joanne in their private little cocoon and have all the stress fucked out of her, but every time she looked at her watch, it was as if time was standing still.

She felt like she was trapped in some weird sci-fi movie where time was out for revenge on humankind by moving slower or standing still whenever they needed it to pass. She felt trapped in an eternity of nothing.

Finally, the end of her workday arrived and Alice walked downstairs to the driver waiting for her outside. She didn't take the same car as Joanne from the office. They didn't want everyone to know they were seeing each other outside of work.

Joanne used the excuse of her tardiness and lack of transportation for using her personal driver. No one dared question Joanne so they got away it.

On the way to Joanne's penthouse, Alice received a text from Joanne. *I'm going to be late. Should be home after seven. J*

Alice felt like the entire world was working against her today. She had been so relieved to finally leave the office and be with Joanne and now she would have to wait some more.

Maybe she could do something nice for Joanne before she got home? Alice asked the driver to stop at her apartment first since she wanted to grab a few things.

When they reached her apartment building, Alice ran upstairs and into her apartment where she quickly pulled open her drawers to look for the white lace negligee she had bought as a surprise for Joanne.

When she arrived at Joanne's penthouse, Alice checked all the kitchen cupboards to find something to cook Joanne a nice meal. Alice was not comfortable to cook with the items she found. Some of the names she couldn't even pronounce, never mind figure out how to use. She decided to go with plan B and put together a charcuterie board.

With plenty of time to spare, Alice decided to relax in Joanne's huge bath tub. She filled the tub with bubbles and closed her eyes as she began to think of all the things she wanted to do to Joanne during their evening together.

FEELING DRAINED after a long day of back-to-back meetings, Joanne walked into her penthouse eager to spend time with Alice. A smile crossed her face as she thought of how hot Alice looked today and how badly she wanted to pull her close and do all kinds of naughty things with her.

Joanne walked around in search of Alice and stopped dead in her tracks when she finally found Alice waiting in front of the fire pit on the deck.

There were flowers and candles everywhere. She had no idea how Alice managed to pull this off in so little time, but it looked amazing. When Alice noticed her, she stood up and Joanne could feel her heart skip a beat.

Alice was waiting in a sexy white negligee. The silky

part was flowy and moving in all the right places while the lacy top barely covered her beautiful breasts. Joanne swallowed hard. "Hi," she managed to get out.

"Welcome home," Alice said as she slowly stalked towards Joanne still frozen in place.

"What is all this?" Joanne asked.

"I just thought I would do something nice for you after the day you had. Come sit, you must be exhausted," Alice said as she took Joanne's hand and led her to the seating area.

"I just wasn't expecting this. It looks wonderful, thank you," Joanne said as Alice removed her sky-high stilettoes.

"You don't need to thank me. Just enjoy it with me," Alice replied as she began massaging Joanne's feet.

"I could get use to this kind of treatment, you know," Joanne teased.

"I don't think that's a good idea, I don't think I could think of ways to surprise you every single day," Alice said.

The foot massage felt so good; Joanne already felt more relaxed. "What would you like me to order for dinner?" she asked.

"No need. I've got it covered," Alice said as she quickly got up from her seat and rushed inside.

Confused, Joanne decided to pour them both a glass of wine while she waited. She heard Alice's tiny footsteps approaching. "Please don't tell me you actually cooked." She knew that Alice was clueless when it came to cooking and didn't have the energy to pretend.

"Not exactly," Alice said as she placed the charcuterie board on the table.

Joanne smiled at her and said, "It looks wonderful, thank you, Alice."

The women sat down and shared their stories about

their weekends while feeding one another from the vast selection of meats and cheeses. Joanne never knew that Alice was involved in volunteer work. She wasn't entirely surprised because she knew that Alice had a kind heart.

When Joanne could no longer fight the urge to touch her, she pulled her in for a kiss. Their kiss started off slow and sensual. Teasing and tasting each other until Joanne couldn't stand it anymore and she took Alice to her bedroom. She had plans that would require her to be comfortable. They had a lot of catching up to do and Joanne didn't want to wait anymore.

After a few hours, both women were left exhausted but satisfied. Alice was lying with her head on Joanne's chest. She was snuggled right in and Joanne smiled to herself. Joanne could hear Alice's breathing slow down into the beginnings of sleep.

"I love you," she heard Alice whisper.

Joanne froze. She didn't know what to do. She could feel her blood turn cold and her heart felt as if it were about to beat out of her chest.

This was not supposed to happen. This was not part of their agreement. They had a good thing going. Why did Alice have to ruin it?

If she loves me, she will just get hurt.

There was something so pure about Alice's love. There was something so pure about Alice. Joanne lay in the bed frozen and waiting for Alice to fall into a deep sleep, watching her beautiful face. She couldn't do this. She carefully got out of bed in order to not wake Alice who was sound asleep beside her. Joanne felt a tear run down her cheek. She wished that she didn't have to do this, but she had no other choice.

Before walking out and closing the door behind her,

Joanne looked at the redhead in her bed for one last time. Her heart was breaking, but she couldn't let this happen.

Loving me would only ever end badly.
Loving her would only ever end badly.

ALICE WOKE up with a smile on her face as she remembered where she was. She reached over to the other side of the bed to touch Joanne, but all she felt was the cold sheets. Quickly her eyes flew open and Alice noticed that she was all alone.

Immediately, she was feeling regret gnawing on her. She knew that she shouldn't have fallen asleep but she couldn't help herself. She got up to get dressed and search for Joanne. Alice was hoping that Joanne wasn't too mad at her.

When she reached the bathroom, she noticed an envelope taped to the mirror. Her name penned in Joanne's elegant handwriting. Timidly, she reached for the envelope and removed the note inside. Something felt wrong. She didn't want to read the words staring back at her.

Alice, this is not working. I'm enclosing a check for six months' severance pay and will provide you with a good reference so you can get another job. Please don't contact me again. Joanne.

The words on the note were blurred by tears that were forming in Alice's eyes. She couldn't wrap her head around it. Was this because she fell asleep in Joanne's bed? How could Joanne end things like this? The least she could have done would be to tell her to her face. Being cast aside with meaningless words and a check made Alice feel cheap.

Was the relationship between them all in her imagination? She felt as if Joanne really cared for her. Clearly, she didn't. Clearly, Alice was just another toy for the wealthy, lonely bitch who apparently got bored of her.

Alice quickly got dressed and stormed out of the penthouse. Downstairs, Joanne's driver was holding open the door for her.

"No, thank you. I will no longer be requiring your services," she said coldly, instantly regretting being rude to the driver.

Alice started walking down the street and flagged down the first cab she could find. When she reached her apartment, she broke down. She couldn't hold back the tears any longer. She cried for hours until she finally fell asleep from emotional exhaustion.

∼

"You wanted to see me, Miss Morgan," Kevin said as he poked his head around her office door.

"Come in," Joanne said without looking up from her computer. "I need you to find me a personal assistant within the hour."

"I don't understand. Is Alice not coming in? Is she sick?" he asked with a frown on his face.

"No. Miss Smith is no longer employed by the company," Joanne said coldly.

"I thought you were happy with her; you two made an excellent team," the HR manager said.

"I don't pay you to think, Kevin. Get me a new assistant now."

Joanne did not feel like explaining herself to anyone.

Why couldn't people just follow instructions and get on with it?

"Of course. I'll have someone for you within the hour," Kevin said as he got up to escape the wrath of Joanne.

Joanne got up to pace in front of her large windows again. She couldn't sleep all night. Joanne didn't want to say goodbye to Alice, but she overstepped her boundaries and Joanne couldn't allow that.

Maybe she should have done this sooner. Sure, Alice was the best assistant she ever had, but there was no way she could look at the redhead every day and not remember the way she made her feel. Joanne told herself that she entertained this fling for too long and that it was for the best. She would dive back into her work, and soon Alice would only be a distant memory—just like all the others.

This is the best way, isn't it?
I have to protect myself, and her, don't I?

14

Max and Alice were lying on the worn-out carpet in Alice's apartment. They were staring up at the mucky green ceiling that was starting to peel.

"This one was number...?" Max asked.

"Six," Alice replied as she sat up to take another sip of wine.

"Alice, six jobs in three months is a new record, even for you," Max said.

"You know me. Always striving to do better," Alice said sarcastically.

"This is serious. You know that your landlord is once again preparing your eviction notice as we speak," Max reminded her.

"I know, Max. I know," Alice said as she emptied her entire glass.

"I don't understand why you just don't use the money Joanne gave you," Max said. "You earned every cent of that obscene amount. You worked hard for it and should be spending it."

"Using her money would just make me her whore. Don't you see that?" Alice never even cashed the check that Joanne left her. It didn't feel right.

"You're not a whore for using her money, Alice. You were her actual paid employee! I can't watch you struggle like this. I can't just sit by and watch you spiral downward," Max said with concern.

"I'll be fine, Max. I'll land on my feet just like I always do."

For a few minutes, the air between them felt thick with awkward silence. Alice appreciated what Max was trying to do and she knew that he truly cared, but she knew she would be okay.

Max cleared his throat. "You know, you never told me what actually happened between you and Joanne. I honestly thought that she could be your happily ever after."

"Nothing happened, Max." Alice did not want to talk about it.

"Alice, you can tell me anything, you know that. It's not healthy to try and keep these emotions in," Max said as he sat up to look at her.

"I can't tell you anything because there is nothing to tell. I fell asleep and when I woke up, I found that she left me that stupid letter with the stupid check."

"That's it? She asked you to leave because you fell asleep in her bed after working your ass off for her and surprising her with a romantic dinner and giving her the best sex of her life?" Max asked, confused.

"Yes. I broke her stupid rule of no sleepovers. That's why," Alice said as she got up to rinse their glasses.

"That doesn't make sense. Not even for a cold-hearted Frosty like her."

Alice had enough. All she wanted to do was get into bed and stay there for as long as possible. "Max, I'm tired. I think I need to get into bed now."

Max sighed as he grabbed his things and walked towards her door. "If you're not going to use her money, the least she could do is give you an explanation, Alice. Good night."

Alice locked the door behind her friend. She switched off all the lights and got into bed fully dressed. She couldn't get Joanne out of her thoughts, but she no longer cried herself to sleep. She was all cried out. She spent most of her nights in bed trying to think back on what went wrong. Her last night with Joanne felt so magical until she woke up to the empty bed and cold note.

The darkness in her apartment matched the darkness that Joanne left behind inside her. Alice knew that she would have to find a way to move on. Her life literally depended on it. She decided that the new dawn would bring her some clarity, and just like so many times before, she would go out into the world and find a job that would keep her from spending the check that stared back at her from her bedside table.

"No, this is not what I wanted. Do you need me to spell it out for you?" Joanne scolded her new personal assistant.

The poor girl broke out in tears and ran out of her office.

This was the seventh new assistant that Joanne had after replacing Alice. The first one didn't even last one day. For the second one, Joanne decided on a fresh-faced pretty boy to ensure she wouldn't be distracted, but he just disappeared during his first work day. After that, Joanne chose only sexy young woman. Each hotter than the previous one. She hoped that having a super sexy assistant would distract her from thoughts of Alice, but for some reason Joanne felt no attraction towards any of them. She was broken. Alice had broken her.

Joanne needed to get some fresh air and grabbed her coat to go for a walk. The streets were loud and crowded, but there was a park close to her office building where she usually found some peace and quiet.

She took a seat on the bench and looked at the people going about their lives. She remembered the time Alice told her about the goat yoga and smiled at the idea of living goats roaming around the park, climbing on the group who was packing up their gear in the distance.

"Joanne?" she heard someone say next to her.

It was Max. Alice's best friend. He was the last person she imagined bumping into.

Joanne got up to greet the man dressed in his yoga outfit. "Hello, Max," she said.

"I don't think I've ever seen you here before," Max said.

Joanne felt uneasy talking to someone who is such a big part of Alice's life. "Yeah, I just needed some fresh air. My office is close by," she said.

"I see. Well, have a good day," Max said as he started to turn around.

"Max?" Joanne stopped him.

"Yes?" he replied, clearly not interested in anything she had to say.

"How is Alice doing?" The question came out before she realized what she said.

"Why do you care?" Max said, shooting lasers from his

eyes. It was clear that at that very moment she was his least favorite person and really, she didn't blame him.

"I'm sorry that I asked, okay?" Joanne replied.

"A cold-hearted bitch like you who kicked someone out of their house and left them without a job just because they fell asleep in their bed does not have the right to know how they are doing without them, okay," Max said. His voice filled with anger.

Joanne looked at him in confusion. "Alice thinks that's why I asked her to leave? Because she fell asleep in my bed?"

"Obviously, since she said you two didn't have a fight so that must be the reason. Or maybe you just grew tired of your new toy? Now, please excuse me, I have better things to do with my time," Max said as he turned around and walked away.

Joanne was left stunned. Was that really why Alice thought she sent her away? She didn't remember saying *I love you*? How could she not remember that? It was those three words that destroyed everything.

In that moment, it felt as if the earth was growing unsteady underneath her feet and Joanne took a seat on the bench once again. It was never her intention to hurt Alice. She had ruined everything. From Max's attitude towards her, she could tell that Alice probably hated her now.

If only Alice didn't say those words. They could still be happy together. What they had was different and more perfect than any other relationship that Joanne ever had, including her marriage. Did she do the right thing? What if she didn't kick Alice out that night? Would they still be happy together?

I love her.

And in that moment Joanne knew what she had to do. She knew what she wanted and she knew how to get it.

ALICE WAS WALKING home after another failed interview. She didn't know what she was going to do anymore. Joanne's uncashed check was looking more appealing every day, but she couldn't bring herself to use the money. She didn't know how much more rejection she could take.

As she entered her apartment building, she was stopped at the stairway by the landlord. "I don't have your money yet but I'll have your rent paid by Friday, okay?" she quickly said.

"That's all well and good but could you keep the noise down in your apartment? There are other tenants here as well, you know. And don't let me catch you subletting or you'll be out on your ass quicker than you think."

"What do you mean by keep down the noise? I wasn't home all day," she asked as panic started to set in.

"Nice try, just make sure that I have my money on Friday," the landlord said before walking away to his own apartment.

Was she being burgled? Slowly, Alice climbed the stairs and stopped at her door to listen. The landlord was right, there was someone in her apartment. She quickly felt around in her bag for her can of mace but then remembered that she left it inside her apartment.

Taking a deep breath, Alice inserted her key and turned it slowly to unlock her apartment. She wasn't sure what she would find on the other side but she couldn't stand outside in the hallway in the hopes of whatever was in there just disappearing.

Alice slowly pushed open the door, readying herself for any possible attackers, when suddenly she froze. She quickly did a double take of the door number on the front of her door because for a moment, Alice thought that she must have walked into someone else's apartment.

Alice was certain that it was still her apartment but it looked so different. Her fear of intruders was overshadowed by curiosity so she walked in to take it all in. She made a slow turn to look at everything.

Every wall was painted in a different color. Bright colors just like she always wanted. This was exactly how Alice always imagined her apartment and she couldn't believe what she was seeing.

"Do you like it?" she heard the familiar voice behind her.

Alice turned around and saw Joanne standing in her apartment. Joanne was wearing white overalls and covered in paint splotches from head to toe. The elegant CEO, who was always perfectly dressed with perfect hair and perfect makeup, was standing in her apartment looking like a paint-covered toddler.

"*You* did this?" Alice asked.

"I remembered you telling me that this is something that you've always wanted," Joanne said with a smile, obviously proud of her handiwork.

"Why?" was the only thing Alice could say, still dumbstruck by the colorful walls around her.

Joanne walked closer to her. For a moment she didn't say anything. "Alice, I'm so very sorry that I asked you to leave that night. I realize now that I should have talked to you instead of just turning you away like that."

Alice was stunned. She didn't know what to say. Her heart was beating faster and she could feel her ears starting to glow. It wasn't like Joanne to apologize for anything.

"That last night together, you scared me, Alice. I sent you away because I was scared," Joanne said.

"Scared of what? I don't understand," Alice said.

Joanne seemed uneasy. Alice knew that it was difficult for Joanne to talk about her feelings, and although she wanted nothing more than to take Joanne into her arms and comfort her, she needed to hear what she had to say.

"That night, while I was holding you, you said that you loved me," Joanne said as she turned her head away to avoid eye contact.

Alice placed her hand against Joanne's cheek and turned her face to look into her eyes. "I do love you," Alice sighed. "Why did that scare you?" she asked.

"I was scared of hurting you and of getting hurt myself, Alice. I was scared of having to sacrifice everything that I've worked for. I was scared that I would end up back in that dark, one-bedroom apartment all by myself," Joanne said as her eyes began to tear up.

"You know I would never expect you to give up anything, Joanne," Alice said.

"I know that now. I guess the thing that I was most scared of was that I feel the exact same way about you," Joanne confessed.

"You do?" Alice asked, stunned by the unexpected confession. She always suspected that Joanne might be fond of her but she never imagined that Joanne Morgan would fall in love with her.

"I love you, Alice Smith," Joanne said.

In that moment, Alice forgot about everything that happened. Joanne's confession wiped the slate clean, and Alice grabbed Joanne to kiss her paint-covered face. She couldn't believe that Joanne repainted her whole apartment single handedly. She couldn't believe that Joanne loved her. She couldn't believe that she came back for her.

Breaking their kiss for some air, Joanne look deep into her eyes said, "Alice, I'll spend the rest of my life making it up to you if you'd let me."

Alice felt her heart swell. "I don't need you to do that, but I would like it if you'd spend the rest of your life with me." Alice had no idea where that came from and tried to take back the words before Joanne could run away. "Just promise me we can do sleepovers this time!"

"Yes, I'd like that very much," Joanne replied, and at that exact moment both women knew that their lives had changed for the better. They made love on the messy paint sheets and both of them never felt closer to the other than at that exact moment.

EPILOGUE

"Guncle Max! You came!" the little girl jumped up and down making the frills of her dress bounce with her.

"Of course I came, silly. I wouldn't miss it for the world. Now where is your sister?" Max said to the little girl.

"I'll get her," she replied and ran down the hallway in search of her sibling.

"Thanks for coming, Max," Joanne said as she walked into the room.

"Like I said, I wouldn't miss today for anything in the world," Max replied. "How do you feel about today? Are you ready?"

"Honestly, Max, I've never been more ready. This is one of the happiest days of my life," Joanne said.

Right at that moment, Alice walked in with a pretty little girl on either side holding both of her hands. "Is everyone ready? We don't want to be late," she said.

"I'll get these two strapped into their car seats. Come

on, hooligans," Max said as the giggling girls followed him to the car.

Joanne walked up to Alice and looked her up and down. "You have never looked more beautiful than today," she said as she gave Alice a kiss on the cheek.

"You don't look too bad yourself," Alice replied.

They both stood in the doorway looking at Max as he struggled with the car seats. Today was the day that the adoption of the twins would be legalized. The thought of twins never crossed their minds when they walked into the agency two years ago but when the file with the photograph of the two little blonde girls opened up in front of them, they knew it was destiny.

"Let me help you, Max, you're doing it wrong," Alice said as she walked towards the car to help Max.

Joanne looked at the scene playing out in front of her. She had everything she never knew she wanted. A beautiful wife who kept her on her toes and two beautiful daughters she tried to spoil any chance she got.

Since the twins' arrival, Joanne hadn't worked one hour more than necessary. She didn't want to spend all her time at the office anymore. She couldn't wait to return home to her wife and girls and listen to the stories they shared of the day's adventures.

Alice smiled back at her from the car. "Come on, we're going to be late," Joanne locked the door behind her and when she reached the car she looked back at their lovely home, with its brightly painted walls, its big lawn and white picket fence. She had found her happily ever after.

CEO SERIES

Thank you so much for reading. I hope you loved reading about Alice and Joanne as much as I loved writing them.

Please do check out book 3 in the CEO series- Serving The CEO.

Austin is blown away when the glamorous and demanding CEO Isabella demands her personal service from the hotel bar. What will Isabella demand from her next?

You'll love this Age Gap, Rich Girl/Poor Girl CEO romance. mybook.to/CEO3

AFTERWORD

Hey! Thank you so much for reading my book. I am honestly so very grateful to you for your support. I really hope you enjoyed it.

If you enjoyed it, I would love you to join my VIP readers list and be the first to know about freebies, new releases, price drops and special free *hot* short stories featuring the characters from my books.

You can get a FREE copy of Her Boss by joining my VIP readers list : https://BookHip.com/MNVVPBP

Meg has had a crush on her hot older boss the whole time she has worked for her. Could it be that the fantasies aren't just in Meg's head? https://BookHip.com/MNVVPBP

Printed in Great Britain
by Amazon